Praise for *Dating Mr. December*

"Ashley's fun, contemporary romance is crafted with humor, a sexy premise, and the intriguing backdrop of the picturesque Lake District."

—*Booklist*

"British author Ashley infuses her debut (the inspiration for Lifetime TV's 2009 movie *12 Men of Christmas*) with humor… Readers will enjoy the breezy style and repartee."

—*Publishers Weekly*

"Sexy romantic comedy… not your typical cozy Christmas tale."

—*Library Journal*

"A delightfully witty and sensual contemporary romance… Phillipa Ashley brings this story to life with her charismatic characters, provocative plot, believable dialogue, deliciously sensual lovemaking scenes, and humor, making this story a must read."

—*Romance Junkies*

"Absolutely loved it!… Wonderful quick and smart dialogue, well placed action… If you like Sophie Kinsella, Jill Mansell, or Hester Browne, you will love this author as well."

—*Book Hounds*

"Sizzling chemistry... Plenty of drama, heartache, and misunderstandings to make this a romance novel with some depth to it... left me feeling satisfied and happy."

—*Luxury Reading*

"Phillipa Ashley writes such sexy characters and dialogue that you'll have inhaled this before you realize you're at the end."

—*Drey's Library*

"Excellent... an exciting romance guaranteed to make you quickly turn the pages."

—*Romance Reviews Today*

"I loved the mix of humor and romance... their chemistry popped off the page."

—*Books Like Breathing*

"Light, fun, and snappy. I am left with the question... where can I get myself a rugged mountain rescue bad boy?"

—*Love Romance Passion*

"Witty romance... with dry humor and candid dialog, I was laughing aloud several times."

—*Book Pleasures*

Wish You Were Here

PHILLIPA ASHLEY

sourcebooks
landmark

Published by Sourcebooks Landmark, an imprint of Sourcebooks, Inc.
P.O. Box 4410, Naperville, Illinois 60567-4410
(630) 961-3900
FAX: (630) 961-2168
www.sourcebooks.com

Originally published in Great Britain in 2007 by Little Black Dress, an imprint of Headline Publishing Group, London

Library of Congress Cataloging-in-Publication Data

Ashley, Phillipa.
  Wish you were here / by Phillipa Ashley.
      p. cm.
  "Originally published in Great Britain in 2007 by Little Black Dress"—T.p. verso.
  1. First loves—Fiction. 2. English—Corsica—Fiction. I. Title.
  PR6101.S547W57 2011
  823'.92—dc22

                            2011004633

          Printed and bound in the United States of America
                 VP 10 9 8 7 6 5 4 3 2 1

For Maureen and Garth

CHAPTER 1

'This one looks promising.'

Jack Thornfield would have given a lot to avoid taking the application form out of his personal assistant's hand. Not that there was anything wrong with his PA, unless you counted a caustic tongue and telepathic powers. He didn't want to look up because he didn't want the woman to see his eyes and just *know*...

'Thanks, Martha, but I've already seen it.'

'Yes, Jack, I know you've seen it, but have you actually looked at it?'

Keeping his eyes on the computer screen, Jack reached out a hand. The form bypassed his fingers and flopped on top of his keyboard: three neatly typed sheets of paper with a passport photo attached.

'She ticks all the right boxes,' said Martha.

He pushed the pages off the keyboard and frowned. A line of redundant *F*s now marched across his email to the head of marketing.

'Maybe. Maybe not.'

'Why don't you take a look at her résumé? It's pretty impressive.'

He flashed Martha a smile he knew she knew was part of his best little-boy act. 'You just want me to get a new product manager to get the operations division off your back. You know, I think you'd let me hire your cat, if you thought it could cope with the Tube in the mornings,' he said.

He also knew that Martha was right. He really did need someone to head up the European sector of his specialist travel company, Big Outdoors, like yesterday. The previous one had met, and married, a crocodile wrangler from Brisbane, all within the space of a month.

'Jack, I have media budgets to finalize by close of play today. Shall I get this Beth Allen in for an interview?'

He cradled his palm around the mouse again. 'Why not? You'll never leave me alone unless I do.'

She shook her head at him in disbelief and he wondered, for the umpteenth time, why he put up with a PA who treated him, mostly, with indulgent disdain. Then he noticed the flawlessly prepared presentation, espresso, and king-size Mars bar Martha had laid on the table in his office. That must be three reasons at least, he told himself.

However, chocolate and PowerPoint skills apart, he still didn't trust Martha absolutely. He didn't think it wise to trust anyone absolutely, not even himself, so he waited a few seconds after she'd left the office, just to be safe. As the door closed with a click, he pressed the 'in conference' button on his desktop telephone and smiled to himself. Let Martha 'Sherlock' Symington deduce what she would from *that*. With a glance at the door, he snatched up the application form and pulled off the clip holding the photo.

Jack blew out a long slow breath. He was holding the girl's face between his fingertips and she was staring back at him out of hesitant eyes. It was a face he would have known not just by sight, but by touch alone. Put him in a pitch-dark cave and he'd remember every last millimeter of it. The contours of that determined chin, the soft fringe of her lashes, that mouth like moist velvet… She looked pale but maybe that was the artificial light of the photo booth. He hoped so. The last time he'd seen her, her cheeks had been burnished a soft gold from the Mediterranean sun, just like the rest of her.

As for the oh-so-serious expression, he told himself not to be too surprised. Everyone knew that 'no smiling' was compulsory now in a UK passport photo. If your mouth so much as twitched at the corners, they slammed your application back, marked 'unreadable.'

He ran a thumb over the picture again and then turned to Beth Allen's résumé. It said she had a first-class degree in modern languages, a masters in business administration, and a gold survival swimming badge. The first two took him by surprise—the Beth he knew was struggling to stay the course; this woman had it in the bag *and* her MBA.

As for the swimming badge… how he'd teased her about that as they'd sat round the fire, drinking beers and eating lamb off skewers, almost too hot to bear in your mouth. 'A *gold* award? I'm impressed. Hey, Beth, maybe I should knock myself out on a rock and fall in a pool, just for you.'

'Maybe you should,' she'd teased back. 'So I can ignore you.' But he'd seen her eyes and known she'd have dived right in, even if her hands had been tied. Now, as he stretched back in his chair, the image slid into his head as easily as cleaving through water. Beth skinny-dipping in a mountain pool, her body shimmering out of focus beneath the surface. Her wet footprints on the rocks, drying out even as he followed them into the maquis, the heathland that bordered the coast.

Even with the hum of the air-conditioning in his office, he could still hear the water cascading down the gully, smell the scent of wild herbs and her warm skin as he pulled her against him and she arched against his body. It almost snatched his breath away, seeming like yesterday, not years ago. He suddenly found himself hauled back to reality by a dull throb in his pocket. Jumping to his feet, he dragged his mobile phone from his trousers, pressed the call button, and barked into it: 'Jack Thornfield.'

'No need to shout. It's only me,' said Martha coolly.

'I wasn't shouting,' he said patiently as she waited for his answer. 'When I shout, believe me, the entire floor will know about it, not just you. Didn't you see my phone was on conference?'

Martha sounded unimpressed. 'It's Miss Allen. I thought you'd want to know.'

'What about her?'

'She's available for interview on Monday afternoon. In view of the urgency of the situation, I took the liberty of booking her into a hotel for the night after the interview.'

He held the phone away from his mouth so his PA wouldn't hear him suck in a breath. 'Yeah. Fine.'

'Shall I schedule a meeting for her with the operations director?'

He paused, gripping the phone tightly, wondering which way to jump.

'Jack?'

'I'll handle it.'

Flicking off the mobile, he stared at Beth's résumé, then pressed a thumb to the desktop phone. 'Martha?'

'Yes?'

'It's probably best if you don't tell Ms. Allen I'm interviewing her. My appointment hasn't been announced officially yet. I wouldn't like it to get out ahead of the press release. Please tell her that Allegra Arnold will be seeing her.'

'Of course.'

He paused, debating whether he should betray weakness at this early stage of his acquaintance with Martha. He'd been in charge for a few weeks now, even if his appointment wasn't 'official' yet.

'Is there anything else?' she asked, as the silence on the end of the line lengthened.

'No, that will be all for now.'

Sitting back in his seat, he looked at Beth's résumé again. He really needed fresh blood in the company, new ideas, and Beth did, as Martha had pointed out, tick all the boxes. It was a shame that, once upon a time, she'd also marked his with a thick black line that he'd never quite erased. Jack sighed at his own weakness. The company needed dynamic new staff, sure, but he was kidding himself if he didn't admit he was keen to see her again.

Rolling up his sleeves, he vowed to get the maintenance team to overhaul the air-conditioning system. Then he turned to the report from his sales director. He hadn't got more than a few lines into it when he started shaking his head. Barely two pages long and reeking of cigarette smoke, the project hadn't even been given lip service. It also didn't contain any concrete revenue-producing ideas for new tours. If that was the guy's idea of a 'comprehensive report,' Jack wondered how many other corners had been cut.

Still, he told himself, it was typical. When he'd accepted the job, he'd known Big Outdoors had a good reputation and was one of the longest-established adventure travel companies in Europe. He'd also known it was going nowhere slowly. New owners had taken over and they recognized it was no longer enough to drift along while competitors were pulling for all they were worth. Their rivals had been busy adding exciting new tours and activities that had chomped into Big Outdoors' market share—which is why Jack had been headhunted from his Californian role to be CEO. He needed staff who were just as enthusiastic as he was about developing new tours and activities. Who could come up with—and make a success of—exciting new packages that would not only be profitable but also set Big Outdoors apart from its rivals again.

He scrunched up the sales report and threw it in the bin. He'd never been much of a diplomat and six years of climbing the corporate ladder in the States had knocked any verbal shilly-shallying out of him. Deciding that the element of surprise might work well with his errant sales director, he pressed the desk phone.

'Martha.'

'Yes, Jack?'

'Can you tell Darius Sanford I want to see him?'

'I think he's in a meeting.'

'Internal or external?'

'Internal, I think.'

'Then tell him to cut it short,' he said firmly.

'I'll do my best,' replied Martha. 'And while I've got your attention, you've had seven calls.'

'Anything I should worry about?'

'I don't think so. Most were people wanting you to buy advertising space or from management consultancies.'

'Thanks, Martha.'

'The only one I couldn't deal with was from a Camilla Reed, who says she's a journalist. She insisted it was personal so I said you'd call her back.'

He felt a smile tilt the corners of his mouth. Camilla was the chief feature writer on a travel magazine called *Voyages*. An über-groomed blonde as glossy and upmarket as the publication she worked on. He could just imagine her demanding to speak to him in her cut-glass accent. He'd met her once in the U.S. and she'd been calling to try and do a 'profile' on him ever since he'd taken over at Big Outdoors.

'OK, thanks. I'll speak to her myself. By the way, Martha. Thanks for the Mars bar. Sweet.'

CHAPTER 2

'Aren't you going to have any breakfast, lass?'

Cookie in one hand, bag in the other, Beth Allen brushed her lips over her father's cheek. 'Sorry—no time,' she mumbled, shoving half a chocolate chip cookie into her mouth while trying to scoop a shopping bag of files from the floor. 'And I wish you wouldn't call me "lass," you make me sound like some hard-done-by girl in a Catherine Cookson novel or *Coronation Street*.'

She suspected he only called her 'lass' to annoy her—and truth be told, she *almost* half-liked it. In a retro-ironic way, that is, and as long as there was no one around to hear.

'It doesn't do, going without proper food at this hour,' grumbled Steve Allen, ignoring her and doing his best to open the door with one hand. Early morning light filtered into the hall as he managed to get it half open. The light only seemed to make his face look greyer than ever. He looked like the old men who played dominoes in the local pub, yet he was at least thirty years younger than them.

Beth was sure he'd aged inside as well as outside in the past few months.

'You should at least have a bit of toast or something…' his voice trailed off but she knew what he was thinking. That he should have got up and prepared something, and felt guilty that he hadn't or couldn't. She shook her head and chewed furiously at the same time, spilling crumbs onto the carpet.

'Dad, I won't starve, and besides, it's too early for black pudding and fried egg. I'll get something later on the train,' she said, swallowing the last of her cookie. Her father looked on disapprovingly as she pushed the door fully open with her bottom. Outside in the yard, racks of bicycles packed the space between the old stone walls. The spring sun was glinting pinkly off the skylights of a lean-to workshop shoehorned in at the far end of the yard—the place that had been home and livelihood for her family for as long as she could remember. Not that she'd spent much time there since leaving for university. She felt a squeeze on her arm and glanced round. Not until recently.

'You will mind how you're going, won't you?'

'Dad, nothing will happen. It's London, not the Sahara or Antarctica. No mountains, no scorpions, no sharks…'

Her father looked doubtful. 'I wouldn't be too sure. Honor's nephew got mugged on the underground last week.'

'I promise I'll be on my guard constantly. No mugger,

scammer, pervert, or Jehovah's Witness will get within ten feet without me noticing.'

'There's no need for sarcasm,' said her dad, frowning. 'Your mum's second cousin is a Witness and he's a qualified civil engineer.'

'He could still be a pervert,' she said, making her dad shake his head in despair. 'Stop fretting, I'll be fine—and now I have to go.'

As she stepped into the cobbled yard, she hoisted her bags high to avoid a rack of trailer bikes whose flags were fluttering in the breeze. 'See you on Friday,' she called at the gate. Her father was leaning against the door frame, almost smiling but not quite.

A horn hooted in the street.

'Don't forget to phone when you get there, madam,' he shouted.

'I promise! Sorry, Dad, I have to go. That's Honor's van—I don't want to make her late for her customers. And don't call me madam, either.'

She walked briskly down the path towards a van whose engine rumbled through the morning silence. It was, her mum would have said, a sight for sore eyes. No other van in the Lake District, or the world, as far as she knew— and she'd been around—had a Holstein cow paint-job. Its driver had one arm resting on the open window, the clutch of silver bracelets on her wrist jangling against the metal.

'Morning, Honor,' she called, still tasting cookie crumbs on her lips.

'Good morning indeed!'

Honor Matthews was scarily cheerful for 6 a.m. In fact, she was scarily cheerful a lot of the time. Beth bent her head to the open window. 'Thanks for picking me up so early. It's a bit of a cheek, me cadging a lift.'

Honor pushed a hand through long blonde hair, streaked with silvery grey. 'Pepper-and-salt,' thought Beth suddenly, recalling one of her mum's favorite phrases. Telling herself getting maudlin twice in one morning wouldn't help anyone, she bit her lip and grinned. 'Daisy's looking well.'

Honor pulled a face and patted the steering wheel. 'Daisy may look well but she does have a slight clutch problem, which means a visit to Frayle's next week, I fear, and a rather large invoice.' She sighed, then smiled again. 'But don't worry about cadging a lift because I'd have been up and about whatever. I'm serving breakfast to a bunch of fabulously hunky firefighters doing the Three Peaks Challenge.'

'Hmm… I agree that's not a bad way to start the day,' said Beth, stowing her bag in the back, careful not to squash the bread rolls. 'Still, it's really good of you to drop me off at the station. It's a bit out of your way.'

'Can't have you getting a taxi. We want you fighting fit and ready for the fray. I'm sure you'll knock 'em dead in London.'

'I hope so. Fingers crossed.'

With a rattle of the clutch, Honor pulled away. Beth glanced up at her little sister Louisa's window. The curtains were still tightly shut, of course—it was horrendously early. It had been Louisa's eighteenth birthday the night before and they'd all had a family dinner. Beth should have had an early night but they'd stayed up late, sharing a bottle of bubbly. Maybe she'd text Lou later, she thought, as Honor turned on the Radio Cumbria news. Gazing out of the car window as they skirted the lakeside road, she watched the sun rippling along the surface of the water as the mist rose.

Beth knew that Honor would have given her a lift whether she had a catering gig to go to or not. An old schoolpal of her mum's, Honor had been a very good friend to the family since Diane Allen had died suddenly when Beth was a teenager. Honor had never tried to replace her mum; none of them would have wanted that. Yet she was invariably there when needed, like a well-loved, if rather eccentric, fixture.

With very little traffic about, they had soon reached the signals at the bottom of the hill to the station. A red light forced them to stop and her eyes inevitably rested on the ranks of shiny BMWs and Audis standing guard on a garage forecourt.

'Frayles,' said Honor.

'Of course,' said Beth.

Nothing disturbed the tranquil, imposing façade of Frayle & Son. There was no little man polishing the windscreens of the cars, no suited and booted salesman trying to persuade a well-heeled couple to part with their cash for the latest model. No Porsche with personalized plate, parked in the space marked 'Reserved: Sales & Marketing Director Only' and no Marcus, standing in the showroom, shaking hands on another deal.

A pang of guilt struck her. Marcus hadn't found out yet that she was running away to London. If he had, he'd definitely have offered her a ride and in something even flashier than a cow-patterned van. He might have tried to persuade her not to leave. Beth was almost sure he might have offered to step in and help out her family financially too. No chance of that, she thought as Daisy chugged up the hill to the little station. She respected herself, and Marcus, way too much to take handouts, however well-meaning.

Marcus was a nice, solid guy. As far as she knew, he never wasted his hard-earned cash on online poker, drank more than the government-recommended limit, or wore a tie that clashed with his Hugo Boss shirt. Plus, on the odd occasion when she'd stayed over at the Grange with him, he'd made sure the burglar alarm was set and always flossed before coming to bed. They'd been seeing each other, on and off, for a few months now. In fact, Marcus was probably the most serious relationship she'd had since Jack Thornfield.

Now where had he sprung from, today of all days, when her mind needed to be cool and businesslike? It must have been... no, she *knew* it was eight years, almost to the day, since she'd last seen him. He'd waved her off on a minibus to the airport in Corsica, wiping away her tears with his thumb, before saying gruffly, 'I'll call you as soon as I get back home.'

At least, that's what she'd always thought he'd said. After all this time, the memory was beginning to shift and become hazy around the edges, a bit like the masts shimmering tantalizingly through the mist on the lake.

'Are you feeling OK?' asked Honor, as Beth wound down the window.

'Fine,' she said brightly. 'Well, maybe a *bit* nervous... It's a big day.'

'Understandable but no need. This Big Outdoors place will be begging you to stay as soon as they meet you. You're staying overnight, aren't you?'

'Yes. They said I could have a night in a hotel before the interview but they can't see me until after lunch and I wanted to be here for Lou's birthday dinner last night. So it seemed a good idea to stay on afterwards instead.'

'Especially if it's free.'

'I didn't like to say no. The woman who arranged it seemed really insistent. I didn't want to make a fuss before they've even met me.'

She turned her face to catch the fresh morning breeze

blowing down from the fells. Jack Thornfield's name had thrust its way into her mind most unwelcomely. She'd stopped Googling his name on the Internet years ago, which was a big step along the road to recovering from being swept off her feet then dumped by him all in the space of three weeks. When he'd left her, he'd taken something with him—her ability to trust—and for a long time afterwards, she'd been as wary of men as a pool she couldn't see the bottom of.

'Um… we're here.'

Honor was gazing at her in amusement and she found they were parked in the lay-by outside the station.

'Oh, sorry. I was on another planet there,' she said.

'I could see that.' She patted Beth's arm. 'They'll be OK, you know, your dad and Louisa. I'll see to that.'

She felt a stab of guilt, realizing Honor was referring to her family. Yet she hadn't been thinking about them at all but about some guy from years ago who should have been long forgotten. Cursing herself, she decided to shove any thoughts of Jack Thornfield into the mental bin marked 'dump.'

'I know you'll take care of them. I really appreciate your help. Thanks, Honor, you're a star.'

'Nothing starry about it. Like I said, it's a pleasure. Now, shall I get your bag out?'

'No, I'll do it. Thanks again.'

Impulsively, she leaned over and kissed Honor on the cheek, then mumbled goodbye and was gone, not looking behind again until she was safely in the station. After her short journey from Windermere to the main line station outside Kendal, she found herself tottering down the aisle of the swaying train in her new heels, a Styrofoam cappuccino in one hand and a breakfast panini in the other. As she mumbled her apologies after lurching into a man in an aisle seat, she wondered how she was going to last the day in the heels. She'd got them in a Faith sale and they'd seemed the kind of 'serious' shoes that she ought to wear for a London interview. Her little toe was already telling her she'd have been better off in her trusty O'Neill wedges. Preferably with sand under her soles and a few palm trees waving nearby.

She slid back into her seat as the train whizzed through countryside and urban sprawl on its way to London. Balancing her coffee on the table, she peeled off the top to let the steam escape and resumed her study of the file on Big Outdoors. Ever since she'd sent her letter, on spec, to their operations director, she'd spent every spare moment on the Internet, boning up on the company's market strengths and weaknesses. Not that she'd expected to get a reply, let alone an interview. Offering her services as a product manager had been a stab in the dark but, she reminded herself, she was desperate. Her stint with a small tour operator company had been going very well until it was cut short by her father's accident.

She tried to memorize the key points in her notes again. They were starred and marked with one of Louisa's fluorescent highlighters. Sisters were useful for some things, she thought, as the first sip of coffee scalded her tongue. She'd noted three main criteria that were considered essential for the role she hoped to get:

1. Recent, extensive, independent travel in Europe, the Middle East, and North Africa—Tick to that box, she thought with a wry smile, although the 'recent' part was a bit debatable.

2. Commitment, energy, and drive—Hmm. Her energy levels were sapping slightly, again due to the events of the past six months. But a big tick to commitment and drive.

3. Ability to forge unique client relationships and deliver outstanding customer service—She sighed. 'Unique' and 'outstanding'? They were typical industry buzz words but they still sounded daunting. All those months at home must have knocked her confidence. She wasn't sure she could be unique and outstanding, but if that's what it took to get this job, she had no choice but to try.

CHAPTER 3

IT WAS MID-AFTERNOON WHEN BETH FOUND HERSELF ON unfamiliar terrain again. She tilted back her head, seeking out the peak of the glass atrium, far above, until she felt dizzy. In front of her was a huge reception desk and a glass lift, straight out of the starship Enterprise. Maybe, she thought, Big Outdoors had a transporter room that beamed people off to their destinations. Maybe they didn't have to get there by plane and ferry, by camel train and elephant, by hiking through the wilderness and gully-bashing.

Like her previous employer, Big Outdoors was a specialist adventure tour operator, but it was in a different league in terms of size. Its flash London offices made it look even more important than it actually was. According to *Travel Trade Weekly*, the company had moved there eighteen months before when they'd been one of the rising stars of their market sector. Since then its rivals had jumped on the bandwagon. In Beth's opinion, the company badly needed an injection of new ideas.

Catching sight of herself in the polished granite of a fountain, she wrinkled her nose. The reflection showed her distorted and unfamiliar. Was this really her? In the sharp jacket, a short skirt, and shoes that were shiny and serious? She flicked a tongue over her lips, tasting the unfamiliar slick of lip gloss. There wasn't much call for Juicy Tubes in a Lakeland village and Marcus had made it plain he wasn't keen on blackcurrant-flavored kisses anyway.

Though her legs felt like jellyfish tentacles, she straightened her back and approached the starship bridge where a young receptionist was intent on a laptop computer screen. She had a purple crop, dozens of bangles, and heavily kohled eyes that made her look like a funky baby Panda. Suddenly Beth felt overdressed in her suit. Maybe her O'Neills would have been a better idea after all…

'Hi there. Can I help you?' said the funky receptionist.

'I have an appointment with Mrs. Arnold.'

'Could I have your name, please?'

'Beth Allen.'

'Cute name,' said the girl, typing it into the computer. 'Short, I mean.'

'Yes. I suppose it is. Short, I mean. Though I have to say I hadn't really thought of it as cute.'

'It is. Easy to spell too,' said panda-girl sagely. 'I mean, when you give people your name on the phone you don't want anything long or weird like Philomena Bottomley or Montague Spraggworthy, do you?'

She felt a giggle rising. 'Definitely not.'

'I mean—like my name. Freya Scott. That gives people a bit of trouble. Not the Scott bit, naturally.'

'Naturally,' said Beth, half wanting to laugh and half wishing Freya would shut up and lead her to the guillotine.

'People always know the Scott, no probs. Cos they've heard of that bloke who went to the North Pole or the poetry guy. No, it's the Freya part that gives them trouble,' she said, rolling her eyes dramatically. 'Dunno what my mum and dad were thinking of. I mean, people think it's some kind of weird made-up name—like Chardonnay or Chanterelle or Jackdaniels or something.'

'Chanterelle? Isn't that a mushroom? And *Jackdaniels*? People don't really call their kids these names, do they?'

Freya looked astonished at Beth's ignorance of such matters. Her reading consisted mainly of *Trail* and *Mountain Bike World*, unless she managed to get a peek at something glossy or scandalous—or both—while she was in the hairdresser's.

'I read it in one of those magazines my mum gets to read in the bath,' Freya went on. 'You see, this woman, she'd had five kids by four different guys, plus the one she didn't know she was having, and she called him Jackdaniels because she'd had sex with the dad in the toilets in All Bar One and—'

Suddenly, Freya curled her tongue over her lip, making the silver stud jiggle. 'Oh flip. I'm going on, aren't I? I keep getting into trouble with Allegra for that. She's our—'

'Human Resources director?'

'Oh… er… Do you know her? Have you come for a job here?'

Beth felt a bit sorry for Freya; she looked so young and worried. She nodded discreetly.

'Oh… er… I'd better shut up then. I thought you were a supplier or customer come to complain about their trip or something. Ah. Here you are. Oh!' She paused. 'Oh, er…'

'What is it?' said Beth, getting worried now.

Freya clammed her black-lipsticked mouth shut then said in a posh voice: 'Nothing. Someone will be with you in a moment. Please take a seat, Miss Allen.'

Beth resisted the urge to ask which one and walk out with it. She doubted if even Freya would understand her sense of humor down here but then again, Big Outdoors did claim to be an *adventure* travel company. Sinking back in the voluminous leather couch, she picked up a travel magazine and flicked through it, trying to look business-like. Better behave, she reminded herself; there was more than her career development riding on this job. Both her dad and Louisa were depending on her, for a start.

'Ms. Allen?'

A tall woman with her silver hair in an immaculate updo was smiling down at her.

'I'm Martha Symington, the managing director's personal assistant,' she said, holding out a manicured hand. 'I hope your journey went well?'

Beth coughed to clear her throat and laid the magazine on the table. 'Absolutely fine, thank you,' she said, shaking hands. She hadn't greeted anyone so formally for months now and it felt pretty strange.

'I hope you had no trouble finding us?' said Martha as Beth struggled to rise elegantly from the depths of the sofa.

'No problem,' she lied, deciding it was better not to mention a slight mix-up on the Tube that had resulted in an unscheduled scenic tour of the London Underground. Not if she wanted a job planning routes along the high Alpine trails.

'This way, please,' said Martha. 'Shall I get Freya to take your overnight bag and keep it in the storeroom? You won't be needing it until later.'

Freya emerged from behind the reception desk. 'Good luck,' she mouthed, raising her eyebrows behind Martha's back. As she took the bag, she hissed, 'You'll need it with him up there.'

She didn't have time to reply or even think about this dire warning. Moments later, she was following the PA across the foyer towards the lift. Martha pushed the button. 'Sorry,' she said apologetically, 'but the management suite is on the top floor, Ms. Allen.'

'That's fine—and please, call me Beth.'

The doors opened onto a corridor. Trotting behind Martha, she tried to read the brass plates on each door they passed. At the end, Martha pointed to a pale beech panel that looked broad enough to admit ten executive directors. She noticed the brass plaque was missing; only screw holes showed where it had been.

'Well, we've finally arrived at the inner sanctum,' said Martha.

'Some sanctum. Mrs. Arnold certainly knows how to choose her office.'

'Ah, but this isn't Mrs. Arnold's sanctum. Mrs. Arnold is at a conference. This,' said Martha rapping smartly on the door, 'is our managing director's sanctum. He'll be conducting your interview.'

Before she had time to reply, a voice thundered through the beech panel.

'Come!'

Beth didn't care too much for the way the word was barked out. It sounded far too dictatorial for her liking. There wasn't even a please, for goodness' sake. Maybe applying for a job at Big Outdoors wasn't such as good idea, with an old ogre like that at the top. Yet Martha was gazing at her kindly, rather like the school secretary had when she'd been hauled up in front of the headmistress for carving graffiti on her desk.

'In you go, then,' whispered Martha, as she dithered, 'and please, don't look so worried. His bark really is worse than his bite.'

As soon as Jack had heard from Martha that 'Ms. Allen' was in reception, he'd assumed the position—the one with his back to the door and his eyes fixed on the city skyline below. He did it partly because he thought it gave him an aura of confidence, and partly because he wanted time to bring his heart rate down to normal and his expectations to zero.

If the truth be told, and Jack always tried to be brutally honest with himself, he'd spent the past week in a complete dilemma. He had no idea what to expect from Beth. He knew his appearance would come as a surprise. It would be weeks before his appointment filtered into the trade press, and as she had addressed her application to the old MD, he was pretty sure Beth wouldn't know he had taken over. As for her reaction to finding him in charge, he knew that could be anything from outrage to indifference. After all, it had been eight years ago since their trip to Corsica—maybe it hadn't meant that much to a nineteen-year-old, maybe he'd been forgotten within a few weeks as Beth moved on to new experiences and new people.

He had to admit that indifference would bother him most. What if she didn't, after all this time, even *recognize* him? He knew he was being irrational because, at one time, he'd prayed that she'd forget him just to minimize the pain he must have caused her.

Checking his watch, he felt warmth on his face as the afternoon sun swung round to the front of the building.

He rubbed a hand across his gritty eyes. He'd woken up at 4 a.m. that morning and hadn't been able to get to sleep again, so he had gone out for a run, trying to make sense of his motives. Did he genuinely want to give Beth a job? Or was he trying to make up for what he'd done to her all those years ago?

'Jack, it's Ms. Allen.'

The rap on the door made him jump.

'Come!' he shouted, then cursed himself. He really hadn't meant to sound like a Roman emperor addressing the plebs. Maybe he needed to get in touch with his feminine side. He called again, more bellow than bark.

'Come in! Please.'

Outside the sanctum, Beth heard the call. Unclenching her fist, trying to ease the tension in her fingers, she pushed the door tentatively. The panel swung inwards, making her blink against the light. A sudden blast of air-conditioning dried out her throat. Her nose twitched as the scent of rich, expensive coffee filled her nostrils.

As her eyes adjusted, she noticed a man standing against the huge floor-to-ceiling windows opposite her. It was hard *not* to notice him—he had to be well over six feet. His broad shoulders were almost straining against the white cotton shirt. His strong back tapered to a lean waist and a rather firm backside. But just as she was telling herself that it was deeply wrong to be ogling bits of her potential new boss, he turned round.

She let out a tiny gasp as the sun blasted in through the window behind him.

Once upon a time, lying alone in bed, sometimes in tears, sometimes twisted with fury, she had planned what she would say if she ever came across Jack Thornfield again. That was years ago and now all of her well-planned responses rushed from her mind as fast as a beck over a crag face.

'Hello, Beth. Please come in.'

She flinched. Jack wasn't shouting now. He said her name confidently and gave her a professional smile as if they'd never met or ever shared anything extraordinary at all.

CHAPTER 4

Seconds later, she was still standing by the door and she still couldn't see Jack properly. Not because of the brightness of the office but because tears were scalding the back of her eyes. Adrenaline was pumping through her veins. The urge to fight or run away was making her feel shaky, light-headed.

'Beth—are you OK?'

She wasn't nineteen, naïve and in love. She'd grown up and got over him and built a life. So why did her legs suddenly feel like ice cream on a hot day? Why was her heart hammering as though she'd just climbed to the top of a cliff?

'I'm going. There's been a mistake.'

Jack was already halfway across the room. 'Hey there. Hold on a moment!' he called, reaching out his hand.

'I think you've got the wrong person.'

'No. No mistake.'

Briefly his fingers rested on her sleeve and she snatched her arm away as if she'd been branded. Jack held up his hands, palms outward. 'I can't stop you from leaving, Beth, but wouldn't it be a shame to do that, now you've traveled all this way? You don't want a wasted journey, do you, not after three hundred miles?'

'I'll live, Jack. All I know is you've got me here under'—Beth was struggling to give what he'd done a name—'false pretenses.'

'I'm sorry if you think I've wasted your time, but you're wrong if you think I lured you here under false pretenses…'

Beth wanted to scream. 'I know you can't possibly want to interview me and I don't know why you asked me, but if it was some kind of whim…'

He shook his head. 'Now, that's not a good pitch, is it? Believe me, I did not get you here on a whim. You sent in your résumé—and yes, I know you didn't know I was in charge.'

'Obviously. Or I wouldn't be here. And that wasn't a pitch, so don't flatter yourself. I've just decided I don't want the job after all.'

'I know what you must be thinking…' he said carefully.

'Do you?' she cried, her voice sounding horribly high-pitched all of a sudden.

'Beth, just for a moment, listen to me. I can understand why you're upset and angry but—'

'Understand why I'm angry? If you can, you'd never have…' Her words trailed off as she teetered on the edge of letting Jack see how much he had once hurt her.

He sucked in a breath. 'Beth, I can appreciate you're upset about what happened between us, but just for a moment, let's forget the past. I need a new product manager and I'm interested in what you have to offer. Your résumé is very impressive,' he went on, quickly back in control, the perfect player as ever. 'So if you're serious about having a job here, you'll have to bite the bullet and stay, I'm afraid.'

Right now, all Beth could think of were the hopes she'd had when she'd set off that morning, all the things that were riding on this time away from her family. Jack had shattered her dreams once before; now he'd let her down again, when it mattered most.

'Jack, I'm going to say this politely and one last time. If you think that getting me down here for some twisted reason of your own is ethical or professional, you're misguided.'

'Beth—'

She ignored him. '*If* you think I want to work for a company whose chief exec treats his employees like you have just treated me, you're out of your mind. I won't be used by you again, no matter how much I might want a job with your company. You can forget it. This interview's over and you can tell your PA *I* ended it. Would you mind moving, please?' she asked, as if he were a stranger blocking her way in the street.

Doubt flickered across his eyes and there was a horrible moment when she thought he might reach out and physically stop her from leaving. Instead, he took a step sideways, leaving her just enough room to squeeze past. Her hand was curved tightly around the handle of the door as his next words, spoken to her back, resonated through her body.

'Are you absolutely sure you want to walk away from this?'

She wrenched open the door and felt warm air from the corridor heating her face.

'I've never been more sure about anything.'

As she closed the door on him, the click seemed to fill the empty corridor. She felt moisture against her cheek and wiped it hurriedly on her sleeve. Then she quickened her stride, her heart racing in dread that Martha might appear and ask her what the matter was. Moments later, she was in the lift, punching the button for the ground floor. The glass cage bobbed, the doors whooshed open, and she was back down to earth again.

Freya glanced up hastily from the computer as she approached the desk, her head held high.

'Would you mind getting my case, please?' she asked.

'Erm... right now?'

'Yes, please. If you could.'

'No problemo,' said Freya, taking a key from her desk and starting to unlock the storeroom. 'How did it go? How did you get on with He Who Must Be Obeyed? You didn't seem to be in there long, if you don't mind me saying.'

Beth used her last ounce of self-control to smile at Freya, wondering how she kept her amazing sense of humor while working for Jack. 'He was called to an urgent meeting so we had to cut the interview short,' she said, not caring that her lie might soon be found out.

'Oh God, what a pain!' exclaimed Freya, her eyes full of concern as she handed over the bag. 'Can't you come back tomorrow?'

Beth seized her case and tightened her fingers round the handle until her knuckles whitened. 'I don't know, but maybe it's for the best. I'm not sure working here is the right thing for me, after all.'

CHAPTER 5

SOMEHOW, BETH MANAGED TO FIND THE HOTEL WHICH HAD been booked for her by Martha. She'd trudged around the West End for who knew how long, gazing in shop windows at clothes she couldn't afford and didn't really need. Thousands of people flowed around her, leaving her stranded as they went about their lives, shopping, doing deals, talking, holding hands.

Wandering the streets had been an escape, she realized as she pushed open the door of her hotel room later that day. While she'd been surrounded by strangers, she'd been able to hold herself together. Pretend she was just another girl up in town for the day on business, hitting the shops on her lunch break, maybe off to a bar later for a night out with the girls.

Now, alone in her hotel room, the façade crumbled to dust. Kicking off the evil heels, she flung herself on the bed and sobbed, not caring who might hear. A hundred questions raced through her mind. What did Jack want by dragging her all this way? What could he hope to achieve? Did he think she'd fall at his feet and be grateful he'd even considered her for the job?

'I hate you, Jack!' she shouted to the empty hotel room. 'I hate you...' The words trailed off into the pillow and finally she abandoned herself to big, loud sobs that weren't only for today's disappointed hopes. She knew, deep down, they were for the past too.

Hours later, Beth woke to find the bed and night stand littered with damp tissues. Her clothes were a crumpled mess; her eyes were gritty and the early evening sun was slanting in through the plate-glass windows. She lay on the bed for a while, trying to find the energy to get up, before fishing her phone out of her bag and reluctantly turning it on. What if Jack had called? Or Louisa had phoned to ask her how she'd got on? What would she say to her sister? She knew they'd be disappointed to hear she hadn't got the job. They'd be stunned if they found out she hadn't even given it a shot. She'd have to lie. But then, she reminded herself, that's what you got from messing with Jack Thornfield.

After a shower, she pulled on jeans and a T-shirt, dug her wedges from the depths of her bag, and closed the door on her room. The concierge pointed her in the direction of the nearest cinema. In the dark, she sat among smooching couples, halfheartedly watching a Bond film with a tray of nachos and a Dr. Pepper.

Back in her room, she flicked on the phone again to find a message from her sister.

Well? Lou x

Beth texted back.

Will have 2 w8 and c B x

Well, she consoled herself, it wasn't exactly lying, was it?

Later as she drifted in and out of sleep, she dreamed she had a writhing Jack strapped to a table in a futuristic laboratory. She was laughing maniacally and aiming a laser gun at his crotch, as a countdown blared out above her head. He was giving her his raised eyebrow look and trying to persuade her not to push the button while the countdown droned on. 'Ten seconds and counting…' All she knew was that the whole world would explode if she didn't zap Jack soon…

'God!'

Her hand slapped down on the phone, which was buzzing fit to burst on the pillow next to her. The clock read seven-thirty and she still hadn't pulled the trigger and blown Jack away.

'Uh…'

'Beth?'

'Um… hello, Marcus…'

'You sound weird.'

'Oh, sorry, I'm under the duvet,' she mumbled, poking out her head. 'And it's um… quite early, really.'

'Yes. Well. I apologize, but I came into work first thing to get some paperwork done before the day starts. We're clinching a deal on a fleet of Audis for an accountancy practice and I won't have a moment later.'

She rubbed her eyes. They felt like sand had been thrown in them. In fact, her whole body felt abraded from the inside out.

'And, of course, I wanted to know how you'd got on with the job,' he said ominously.

Her heart sank. Oh God, he knew…

'You see, Beth, I called round to the bike shop last night. Your dad told me you'd gone to London for an interview. I tried you last night, but your phone was switched off.'

She felt like crawling into a hole. No wonder Marcus sounded so distant. He must be furious with her for just taking off, and she couldn't say she blamed him. She knew she should have discussed her plans with him—except she'd already guessed what his reaction would be. None of that mattered now she'd blown her chances out of the water with Jack. She propped herself up on one arm. 'I'm really sorry. I know I should have told you I was coming down here.'

'It would have helped,' he said deliberately.

'I was going to tell you, but… I didn't want to upset you.'

'Actually, not knowing was worse.'

'We'll talk about it when I get back, I promise,' she soothed, about to put him out of his misery and confess she'd decided against the job anyway.

'So where were you last night? With them?'

'I… I went to the cinema,' said Beth, propping herself up on the pillows. 'To see a Bond film,' she added unnecessarily.

There was a silence on the end of the phone.

'Well?' he said.

'Well what?'

'How did you get on? Have you got the job?'

'Erm… not exactly.'

She almost heard the relieved sigh. Poor Marcus. 'I have to say I'm glad, actually. So you'll be back home tonight?'

She couldn't blame him for being annoyed and upset. She should have trusted him with her plans but there was something about the tone of his voice—the way he expected the answer to be yes—that was making her hold back.

'You don't need to take this job, of course,' he went on as she hesitated. 'I know why you're doing it and you know I could help you out.'

Dismay flowed through her. Marcus meant well, but this wasn't what she wanted. She didn't know what she wanted, but a choice would have been good. Suddenly, she was no longer absolutely certain what that choice should be.

'Beth, are you sure you're not ill or something?'

'I'm fine,' she said with a sigh. 'It's just early. I'm not thinking straight and I haven't slept well.'

'Guilty conscience?'

'Air-conditioning.'

'Hmm. So, I'll collect you from the station about 8 p.m.? I believe that's the train your dad said you'd planned on taking? I should be all done with the new clients by then.'

'Well, no. Actually, I'm not sure when I'll be home, Marcus,' she heard herself saying.

'Why not?'

She crossed her fingers and hoped a thunderbolt wouldn't strike her down. 'Because when I said I hadn't got the job what I actually meant was that they haven't interviewed me properly yet.' She felt sick even as she said it. 'The managing director was called away to an emergency, and they asked me if I might be able to go back later today and—'

'That's very inconvenient. Bloody rude too, in my humble opinion.'

'Yes, it is. Very. But it can't be helped and… oh, Marcus, I want this job.'

It wasn't a lie, she acknowledged even as the words slipped out. She did want it. She wanted it a lot. Because if she didn't get it, she was letting Jack win. She was allowing her feelings for him to ruin her chance of a great career, the chance to help her family out, to be independent. By running away, she was allowing Jack to control her.

Marcus's voice came again, sounding tight and annoyed.

'Forgive me, Beth. You think you *need* this job. We'll talk more about this when you get home. I still say there's no need for it. Call me when you get to the station.'

Sighing, she ended the call. She could just picture him, shaking his head, annoyed at her, exasperated but indulgent. Marcus was the type of man who didn't think a woman should shoulder the responsibility of a household. He'd always made it plain that was a man's job. He didn't exactly think she should be tied to the kitchen sink, but she knew he'd rather she dabbled at something than took on a demanding career.

She sat on the bed, surrounded by scattered clothes, empty wrappers and bottles from the mini-bar. Was this the mess that was her life? She'd come down here to get a job she knew she deserved to have. To help her family. And what had she done? Allowed Jack Thornfield to turn her dreams upside down again.

As the digits on the bedside clock rolled to 11 a.m., Beth found herself still perched on the edge of the bed. A cup of cold coffee stood beside her and little balls of paper littered the duvet where she'd rehearsed and discarded what she was going to say.

Her finger hovered above the green 'dial' button on her phone. Outside a car backfired, making her heart thump harder. She took a deep breath, pushed the telephone symbol, and pressed the phone to her ear.

'Good morning. Jack Thornfield's office.'

'Um… Good morning. It's Beth Allen. Is that Martha?'

Martha sounded concerned. 'Ah… Beth. Are you feeling better? Jack said you felt unwell during the interview and had to go back to your hotel. You should have called me. We could have had the company nurse take a look at you.'

'That's very kind of you but it's OK. It was just a migraine. I'm feeling fine now.'

Her heart flipped. She'd wondered just how Jack had explained her sudden disappearance from the office. Had he deliberately left the door open for her? Did he know she might call back? Or was he just protecting himself?

'Would you like to rearrange the interview?' said Martha.

'Is that possible?' she asked, hardly daring to hope she could get the meeting rescheduled via Martha without even speaking to Jack.

'Well, let me take a look at his calendar. Hold on a moment, please.'

She held her breath in suspense. Once she'd made up her mind after Marcus's phone call, she'd become as frantic to have another chance as she had been to blow the first away. She wanted the job; she sure as hell was desperate for the money, and, it was no use denying it, she wanted to show Jack she was over him. Perhaps, a voice whispered to her as she waited for Martha, she needed to prove it to herself.

'Hello, Beth.'

At Jack's voice, her stomach whooshed and all her rehearsed replies fluttered from her mind.

'I was hoping we could talk?' she managed.

There was a pause. 'Yes. But it will have to be later. I've got a conference for most of today. I'll be back about six. Is that too late?'

She knew she would have to get a later train, but it couldn't be helped now. 'No. I mean, yes. That's OK.'

'Six, then. My office. Come straight up.'

'Yes,' she said, her heart racing. 'Is this a formal interview?'

'Do you want it to be?'

'Yes. Yes I do.' Her throat felt dry suddenly. She caught sight of the pieces of paper that had slithered onto the carpet. 'Jack, we have to get something very clear first.'

'Say it, then.'

'I want you to interview me as if you've never met me before. As if I were just another candidate. No favors, no special treatment.'

There was a silence of a few seconds that echoed round the hotel room.

'I wouldn't dream of doing anything else.'

The line went dead as she sat, trying to make sense of the roller coaster ride of events and emotions of the past twenty-four hours. She thrust her phone in her handbag, crossed to the window, and stared out over the London skyline. However it had happened, she'd got what she wanted: a second chance at the job, on her terms.

CHAPTER 6

BETH SPENT THE DAY WANDERING AROUND THE NATURAL History Museum (free), window-shopping in Oxford Street (also free), and sitting in Starbucks (almost free, if she made a latte and granola bar last an hour). When she finally pushed her way into the Big Outdoors foyer, Freya was not on reception; instead, a security guard waved her up to Jack's office. This time, Beth barely had time to lift her hand to knock before he opened the door. He couldn't have been back from his conference long, she guessed, because he still had his suit jacket on, complete with security pass pinned to the lapel.

He stood well back as she stepped into the room. 'I'm glad you decided to give us another try,' he said, before gesturing to a chair opposite his desk.

He waited for her to sit down before settling into a big black leather chair.

'We got off on the wrong foot yesterday. Do you want to rewind?' he asked as she tried to appear cool and in control.

She hesitated. He seemed to be holding out an olive branch.

'Maybe I was a bit hasty yesterday,' she said after a short but painful silence.

'Maybe I should have warned you.'

'Yes. I think you should have.'

He nodded. 'In hindsight, yes. And I apologize.'

'Me too. For walking out and hurling abuse at you.'

He gave her a brief smile. 'Don't worry about the abuse too much. I've had worse. Now, let's start again from the beginning, shall we?'

The beginning, she could have told him, had happened eight years before, but she smiled back, just as briefly. He shrugged off his jacket and hung it over the back of his chair, and she busied herself unpacking notes from her briefcase. He loosened his tie and undid the top button of his shirt and she found herself comparing him with the man she'd fallen in love with. When they'd first met, he'd had thick dark hair that was always flopping into his eyes, surfer-style. Now his hair was cropped almost military-short, which somehow made him seem harder. Beneath the tan, she also thought he looked tired.

'Was your conference the *Travel Trade Weekly* event? Did it go well?' she asked, when they'd both run out of things to occupy their hands with.

He smiled. 'In some ways. If I wanted to know how well our competitors are doing by taking our ideas and developing them, it was a great conference.'

She took it as a cue to start her pitch. So far, he seemed to have taken her warning about keeping things professional to heart and she was grateful. 'I've been doing some research,' she said, clearing her throat. 'If you don't mind me saying, I think you're missing an opportunity with some sectors of the market.'

Jack folded his arms. 'Possibly.'

'You're still number one in the student and gap year sector, but I think you should develop some of your traditional packages for the more mature market.'

He nodded. 'That's interesting, because we've already started moving in that direction.'

She wasn't sure whether she felt disappointed or pleased that her plans had been anticipated. One thing she did know—Jack wasn't going to make things easy for her. She knew he liked pushing people. When they'd first met, he'd persuaded people on the trek to do things they'd sworn they'd never do. But she didn't know him anymore. She handed over some sheets, stapled together and slotted into a plastic wallet. 'I have some proposals here, if you want to take a look.'

'Thanks. We'll discuss these in a minute, if that's OK,' he replied, picking up her résumé from the desk, lifting the top sheet and studying it for a moment.

She knew they were circling around each other, both wanting to keep things strictly professional, both sensing the other's mood. She felt a little twist in her stomach.

Any good interviewer would have picked up on the nuances; it wasn't because they'd once known each other.

'I had another read through your résumé during a break at the conference. It's quite impressive,' said Jack.

'Only "quite"?'

'It's a great résumé, but we'll come to that in a minute. I need to make something clear first. You do know I only have a vacancy for a temporary position? It's with our European sector as a Product Manager. If you join us, it will only be for six months. I've got someone coming back from maternity leave late in the year and we'll be fully staffed again.'

'Of course. That suits me perfectly.'

'OK, then. First things first. Why did you choose to send your résumé to Big Outdoors?'

'It would be a unique experience to work for a successful company,' she said firmly.

'Hmm. Working for us would be a unique experience, I agree, but if you don't mind me saying, I'm not totally convinced by your reply.'

Inwardly, she agreed with him. Her reply had been a bit hackneyed and if Jack had been any other potential employer, he might already have been striking her from his list as too unimaginative.

'It's an up-and-coming company…' she went on.

He raised an eyebrow and an ironic smile twisted his mouth. 'Even with our competitors encroaching on our territory and a new chief exec?'

'I'm convinced those issues won't affect the company's success. In fact, with an ambitious new managing director, the business should go from strength to strength. Not that I knew you were in charge when I applied.'

'It hasn't been announced—officially—yet. The press release goes out next week,' he said smoothly.

'I check the trade press regularly. I didn't see you in it,' said Beth.

'You wouldn't. I've been in the States, working as ops director for a travel firm out there. Big Outdoors has been courting me for some time but I've kept a very low profile. Anyway, let's focus on you. Your résumé *is* very interesting. On the other hand, you haven't taken on a role this big—with a company this major—before.'

'No, but I can bring energy and a fresh approach to the role,' she declared, noting the way he'd steered the conversation back to her. 'I did handle a similar role with Trailburners for three years. Take another look at my résumé and see what I've been doing recently.'

Flipping up the top sheet, he scanned the page. 'I need someone who can devise and deliver some new packaged products that will produce revenue. Your ideas about focusing on a more mature and affluent market are great in principle but we'll need to do our research on them thoroughly to convince travel industry clients to offer them.'

'I know that there would be a lot of work to do at both the supplier and client end,' she said, feeling the adrenaline stirring. 'If I got the role, I'd envisage being very proactive. Really get out there and test run the tours, build links with overseas operators, negotiate hard on terms, let them know what we expect of them and that we're prepared to work as real partners to help them develop the perfect package for guests.'

She suddenly became aware of his eyes on her, intent, a slight smile on his lips. 'I'm sorry if I'm gushing, but I just get a bit carried away. It's the way I did things in my previous role and it brought results.'

He smiled more broadly. 'It's OK. Enthusiasm is one thing we do need.'

'You know I helped Trailburners increase their market share by fifteen percent,' she added, sensing he was impressed.

'That's good. Now they have a two percent share to our thirty.'

She was undaunted. 'It's a start. I know Trailburners is a small outfit compared to a major player like Big Outdoors, but I have ambition and energy…' and, she wanted to add, there can't be that many people with my experience interested in a temporary contract.

'You've convinced me of your commitment, but what I want to know, Beth, is what are you doing right now? It says here you're taking a sabbatical. That could mean anything from working your way round the world to twiddling your thumbs at home.'

'I do *not* twiddle. I wouldn't know how to.'

Jack put down her résumé, leaned back in his chair, and folded his arms. 'What exactly have you been doing since you left Trailburners? Climbing? Guiding?'

'Organizing walking tours for families, middle-aged couples—ramblers, birdwatchers, you know the sort of thing. I know it doesn't sound that impressive, but actually it's been highly relevant experience. Double income couples with no kids, families with teens, older people— they all want a taste of adventure and they have cash and time to do it. And I've been doing my homework; you'll see there are some figures attached to my résumé.'

'OK, I'm impressed.'

She gritted her teeth. 'Well, I haven't just been twiddling.'

'I can see that,' he said rolling his pen between his fingers. 'Beth, I'm not doubting your credentials and I like your ideas, but I do have other candidates in mind.'

'Oh…'

Here it comes, she thought, this is the part where he told her 'thanks, but no thanks.' Her stomach plummeted but she sat up straight, determined not to let him see how disappointed she was.

Jack dropped his pen on the desk. 'I won't prolong your agony any longer. I *do* have other people in mind, but I'll be frank. I haven't invited them for interview. I've every confidence you'll do a great job for us.'

Her stomach zoomed to the top of the building. 'Really?'

'Rule number one. Don't look so surprised when someone offers you what you think you don't deserve.'

'I do deserve it!' she burst out.

He laughed. 'Beth, relax. The job's yours.'

Any other time, any other place, she would have felt like jumping for joy. The part of her that cared about Louisa and her family was jumping. But the other part felt apprehension at the prospect of spending six months as his employee. She couldn't suppress the sense that he'd done her a favor, no matter how much she knew she could handle the role. That made her beholden and answerable to him.

Jack moved to the front of the desk and held out a hand.

'Before we shake hands I do have one condition, though,' she said, her heart racing.

Confusion flickered across his eyes, but she pressed on. 'I am your employee now and I want to be treated as only that. I want us to behave as colleagues. And…'—she didn't know if she dared say this but she had to, no matter what it cost her—'I'm really grateful for the opportunity to work here, but I never ever want us to discuss the past. What went on between us is history and I'll be straight out of the door if you even mention it.'

'Beth—'

'Jack, that's it. I don't want to speak about it. Ever. Those are my terms.' She held out her hand and hoped it was steadier than it felt.

His fingers closed around hers firmly. 'I suppose I have no choice. It's a deal.'

The look that crossed his face could have been remorse or guilt, but Beth didn't know and told herself she didn't want to know. All that mattered from now on was the future: hers and her family's.

'We won't speak of it, then, if that's truly what you want.'

'It is.'

'Then you'll be relieved to know I haven't the slightest intention of treating you any differently to anyone else on my staff. If that means bawling you out in front of them,' he added, grinning, 'I'll do it without a second thought. That's a promise.'

She felt shaky inside, but returned the joke—at least, she hoped it was a joke. 'I'm glad to hear it. If you're going to give someone a bollocking, I say at least do it properly.'

'Agreed.' He smiled. 'And playing by your rules, if you want me to treat you like any other employee, you shouldn't have any problem with coming for a celebratory drink with your new boss.'

CHAPTER 7

Ten minutes later, Beth experienced the bizarre situation of being ushered into a bar by a man who, twenty-four hours before, she'd never expected or wanted to see again in her life. Tucked away up a side street, the place Jack had chosen was buzzing even at this early hour. As they made their way inside, the buzz of voices rolled over her. Only on a weekend at the height of the tourist season were bars ever this busy back in the Lakes.

She hunted down a seat while he fought his way through the power suits. Fortunately, a couple had just vacated a two-seater in a corner and she slipped onto it, squeezing her case between the wall and couch. She'd had misgivings about accepting his invitation and had then relented, reasoning if they couldn't start to behave in something approaching a normal way, there was no hope for a future working relationship. A shiver ran up her spine as she thought about what that concept really meant. In a day, the past had not only caught up with her, but crashed down on her like a great big wave. After eight years apart, they were going to see each other virtually every day.

'What time's your train?' he asked, returning from the bar with a glass of Pinot Grigio for her and a Cobra beer for himself.

'In a couple of hours,' she said, shuffling along the two-seater. He sat down beside her, barely a hand's span between them. Close-up, she got a proper look at the new Jack. Was there the odd grey strand among his dark hair, she wondered, or was she imagining it? She certainly wasn't imagining the tiny lines fanning out from the corner of his eyes. At least they were still the same, not quite blue, not quite black, like slate after rain.

In reaching for her glass, her arm bumped against his, spilling a few drops of wine on his fingers.

'Sorry. It's a bit of a crush in here, but everywhere will be the same, I'm afraid,' said Jack, sucking Pinot Grigio from his fingers.

'Is it always this busy?' she asked, putting the tremor in her hand down to ebbing adrenaline.

'Pretty much. You'll hardly be able to get through the door in half an hour. Everyone's dropping in for drinks before they brave the commute.'

'You too?'

'No. I only live a couple of blocks away,' he said, raising his beer bottle to her in a toast. She held her breath.

'*Slainte.*'

'*Slainte*,' she murmured, taking refuge in a gulp of Pinot, knowing that the last time she'd heard that toast had been round a dying campfire in Corsica. Most nights they'd toasted the group they were trekking with before slipping away to talk, to kiss, and, finally, to make love. It had been during her first vacation from university, a trip she'd been forced to go through with after a friend had dropped out. She'd arrived at Figari airport, knowing no one. Jack, the trek leader, had sought her out, made her feel at ease. That part, at least, had been his job. A job he was still doing now, perhaps even more skillfully.

'So why did you leave Trailburners last year?' he asked, setting the bottle back on the table.

She forced herself to separate the man sitting here in suit and tie from the one she'd once followed, naked, into the maquis. Otherwise, she was never going to get through the next few months.

'I had no choice but to come home because Dad and Louisa needed me. Dad had an accident, you see.'

Jack shook his head. 'Jesus, Beth. Why didn't you say so at the start? What kind of accident? Is he badly hurt?'

'He's on the mend—slowly—and I didn't want to get into this at the interview because I didn't want to play the sympathy card. I don't expect you to employ me out of pity, Jack. I just want to help out my family. They need me.'

'You needn't worry about the sympathy part. You got

the job on your own merits, and as for your family, they're lucky to have you, I'm sure. Now, tell me what happened.'

'I—I'm sure you don't really want to hear the whole saga. I mean, it's irrelevant to the job.'

'But not irrelevant to our working relationship. I'm not an ogre. I do care about what happens to the people I work with.'

She hesitated, wondering just how much to tell him.

'Come on, you've started now.'

His eyes, fringed with thick dark lashes she'd once envied, were full of concern. He was still so good at drawing you out of yourself.

'He was in a mountain bike crash on Hard Knott Pass last summer, coming down a one-in-three slope. We're not sure exactly what happened—maybe his brakes were dodgy but that doesn't seem very likely.' She shook her head and allowed herself the small luxury of a smile. 'It was ironic, really. Dad's paranoid about safety so maybe he just got a bit overconfident on a bend. Whatever caused him to come off the bike, he messed himself up totally.'

Jack winced. 'It sounds like a nightmare scenario. I can only imagine the damage he's done to himself. A guy I used to work with came off a trail in Yosemite. He was off work for six months but I suppose he was lucky to get away with that… like your dad?'

'I wouldn't be exaggerating if I said he's probably lucky to be alive, considering the speed and the gradient and what he connected with.'

'How's he coping now?'

'Well, compared to the state of him when they airlifted him to hospital, OK. I suppose. OK-ish. He had various broken bones, a few ribs went, a smashed jaw, severe concussion, lacerations…'

Jack looked in pain himself as she named some of his injuries, making them sound like a shopping list. No shopping list, she reminded herself, had ever caused so much pain. She'd never forgotten the shock, like a sledge-hammer to the body, when she'd seen her father lying in intensive care, wired up to machines and drips, almost invisible beneath tubes and wires and dressings. Until that day she'd thought Steve Allen was a big man, but he'd been diminished somehow by the machines, the paraphernalia that was keeping him alive.

'He spent months in hospital, then the community nurse was visiting every other day and he still has physio once a week. It's been… an experience.'

'Beth, I am sorry.'

She shook her head, aware she'd been sitting, lips compressed together, tensed up. She'd told the tale to so many people over the months, but telling Jack was different. More difficult, somehow, especially as he was being so sympathetic—so damn nice.

'Do you want another drink?' he asked suddenly. She glanced down. Her glass was empty.

'I shouldn't but… are you having one?'

'Yes. I'm not driving anywhere tonight. I'll have another beer.'

'A small glass of the same, please, then.'

When he got back, he had two glasses.

'I decided to join you with the wine. You're sure you're OK for time?'

'Yes. I'm fine.'

'You were telling me about how your dad's getting on…'

'Much better now. He's still on crutches—on a good day—in a wheelchair on some. I had to leave Trailburners to help look after him and run the business, you see.'

'Is that the cycle hire place in the village?' said Jack. 'Next to the post office, opposite the White Hart? "*Wheels on Fire… burn up the territory.*"' He smiled. 'That was it, wasn't it? Your tag line?'

Beth nodded, wondering if he was mocking her. Their silly slogan was way over the top for a family firm in a Lakeland village. But she studied his face and was sure he was sincere in this at least. A snare of emotion tightened around her chest that he had remembered her tales.

'You must have worked hard to keep the place going,' he went on. 'Trying to run a business is no picnic for anyone these days and with the accident too, life must have got bloody impossible.'

He was right. It had been hard. Her mum had died when she'd been barely in her teens, leaving her dad to care for two young girls. It had been a struggle but they'd managed until lately.

'The business has suffered, of course it has. Some of the locals rallied round and they were fantastic. They all did shifts in the shop at first but it couldn't go on forever. They have lives too. Dad was in hospital for four months and now he's not so mobile. He gets a bit down at times and who can blame him? They needed me so I left my job and went home. That's it. I should be grateful. He's lucky to have got away with what he did. We didn't even know if he'd ever wake up at one point.'

'I'm truly sorry this has happened to you, Beth,' said Jack.

'It's OK. It's just—things are a bit tight.'

'So basically, you wanted this job so badly because you need the money?'

'Not for myself. Not even for Dad. We're getting by, just, with the guided walks and the shop. It's for Louisa. It's her I really need the job for.'

'Your sister? Don't tell me she's in trouble too?'

Beth felt a smile tilting the corner of her mouth. All she'd done so far was pour out a tale of woe. Now, at last, she had something to be pleased about.

'On the contrary. Louisa's doing really well. That's the problem, she's been accepted by a top performing arts school,' she said ruefully. 'A really expensive one, but there's no way Dad or I are going to let her pass up a chance like this. No way. I want her to have the chance, but I need to earn a decent amount.'

His eyes were serious. 'I can understand that. Opportunities like that don't come along very often and you're right to want to help Louisa. If it were my sister— or my daughter—I'd want to do the same. Who's helping your dad out while you come down here?' he asked.

'Well, he's on the mend, and he can do a bit of pottering around in the shop, but he has Louisa to help now. Her study leave starts at the end of the week and the course at the drama school doesn't kick off until the autumn. So it's the ideal time for me.'

'What about accommodation? Where are you going to be staying when you're working for us? Life down here can be pretty expensive.'

She smiled. 'A relative has said I can house-sit for her. She's letting me have her flat in Camden Town while she visits her daughter in Australia.'

'Camden Town, eh?' said Jack, raising his eyebrows. 'You shouldn't be late for work, then. I was wondering how you were going to manage with your bike on the M6.'

His joke wasn't that good, and she knew it was probably nervousness, but they both thought it was so funny they laughed out loud.

It was a while later, as Jack went outside to take a phone call, that a strange thing happened. The theme song from *Titanic* began to drift into Beth's head above the buzz of the bar. She fumbled inside her bag. Louisa had been threatening for weeks to send a cheesy ringtone to her phone and now she'd obviously gone and done it, the little minx. She'd pulled out an envelope, an underground map, a free voucher to a new vodka bar, and a Juicy Tube lip gloss before she saw it, glowing and warbling in the depths.

'Louisa!'

'Hi, Beth. Are you OK? You sound a bit… weird.'

'I'm fine. I'm in a bar! I just couldn't find the mobile. Just what have you been doing with the ringtone?'

'Beth. Chill. It's only the *phone*.'

She could almost see her sister rolling her eyes in exasperation. She was supposed to be the uptight one. Louisa was, to use her favorite expression, chilled. So chilled she had a blithe confidence that the money would be found, somehow, to send her to drama school. Despite all that happened to their family, Louisa still had that glorious gift, the naïve optimism of youth, and Beth didn't want to enlighten her.

'Is anything wrong? How's Dad?' she asked.

'Not *too* bad. A bit crotchety, but what's new? I thought if you had some good stuff to report he might cheer up…' she paused again. Beth could picture her, lying on her bed or a floor cushion, her iPod trailing. 'Beth,' she went on, 'Marcus has been here again. Dad took him in the front room. I hung about outside the door but I couldn't work out what they were saying. He seemed pissed off you weren't here, though.'

Beth didn't blame him. Poor Marcus, he didn't deserve her. 'I know. I've already spoken to him, so don't worry about it now, I'll talk to him when I get home. I've got some news. I got the job.'

'Yay! You rock, Beth!'

'Thanks, Lou-lou.'

'See you later, then?' said Lou.

'My interview overran a bit so I'm going to be really late back.'

'Me too. I'm off out.'

'On a date?' asked Beth, repacking her bag as she talked.

'Might be…' said Louisa.

'Going to tell me who?' she asked, distracted by the envelope that had fluttered under the table.

'Just some guy from the boat club. Hey, I have to go. Sarah's coming round to do my hair. Love you lots. Mwah.'

'You too, mwah,' laughed Beth, turning off her phone. Reaching down, she picked up the envelope, pulled out the ticket inside, and closed her eyes in disbelief. When she opened them, Jack was pushing his way through the drinkers towards her.

'Sorry about that. Robin Brinton's office, important potential client,' he said as he reached her and sat down. 'Everything alright?' he asked suddenly.

She held out the ticket. 'Not really. I think I'm about to miss my train.'

CHAPTER 8

'WE CAN STILL MAKE IT IF WE GET A MOVE ON,' CALLED Jack, pushing his way through the scrum of drinkers towards the door. Dragging her case behind him, he half ran with her towards the nearest underground station.

'We might do it!' he called from a few yards in front. Then he stopped suddenly and she found herself almost falling into the back of him. The entrance to the station was cordoned off with thick yellow tape. Dozens of people were milling about outside, talking frantically on their mobiles. Overhead, a police helicopter chopped through the sky.

'Sorry, sir,' said a policeman, hands outstretched as Jack made his way to the tape, still pulling her suitcase. 'We have a major incident. You'll have to move back.'

'What about the mainline stations?'

The policeman shook his head at her. 'I wouldn't bother. Nothing's moving in London tonight.'

'Come on. It's no use,' said Jack, steering her away from the underground station to a side street.

She put a hand to her cheek. It was warm and glowing, and not only because of their dash through the streets. 'Are you sorry you took me on now? I can't even catch a train home,' she said.

'You won't be the first or the last travel expert to miss a connection—but you know that,' he said, not unkindly. 'Besides, who could have predicted this would happen?'

'I still feel like a total prat.'

'Forget it. Let's just get you sorted out for tonight. Can you stay with your relative in Camden? I'll walk you there. It's a bit of a hike, but we could do it,' he offered as Beth took her case from him.

She shook her head. 'Not until next week. She has tenants in until the weekend. I can hardly descend on them. I'll have to try and get a hotel room.'

Her eyes took in the chaos around them as Jack checked his phone. 'The network's overloaded. What about yours?'

'Same.' She nodded, looking at her screen.

He blew out a breath. 'OK. Plan B. Let's use the landline in my apartment. It's only around the corner. I have a list of hotels back there too.'

'We might be lucky to get a reservation if we get a move on,' she said, still kicking herself.

'Sure. We can try.'

Horns hooted and sirens screamed as he led her along the pavements, still buzzing with office workers, shoppers, and early evening diners. A few yards on, he stopped outside an entrance door and, minutes later, they were walking into Jack Thornfield's apartment, and then she was sitting on his sofa, waiting while he phoned round the hotels. Any minute now, she'd wake up in hospital and be told she'd been in a coma for the past eight years. Or that they had finally invented a transporter beam and she was the first guinea pig, and the coordinates had gone wrong and landed her in her ex's bachelor pad by mistake.

Sadly, her eyes told her the situation was all too real. To the left, a bank of windows overlooked the streets, the sirens muffled by triple glazing. At one end of the huge open-plan space was a funky chrome kitchen, as clinical as an operating theatre. Opposite her hung a vast Ansel Adams print of Yosemite National Park, the only sign of the natural world.

'Well, I've tried a total of nine hotels but there was nothing doing, I'm afraid,' said Jack, returning from his study with a rueful expression on his face.

She sighed. 'It's not surprising, I suppose. Half of London will be hunting down a room tonight. Thanks anyway.'

'Do you want to try any more?' he asked flicking on the TV. 'Though looking at that lot, I shouldn't hold out any hope.'

Sky News flashed into life on the plasma screen. Early reports were hinting that the incident might have been a sick and elaborate hoax. No one seemed to have been injured, but the whole transport network was in chaos, roads gridlocked. It looked like nothing much would move until the early hours.

'I don't think there's a lot of point, but thanks for trying anyway.' The situation was beginning to crystallize in her mind. She had nowhere to stay, no prospect of transport until the early hours.

'Look, I know this might not be an attractive proposition, but, in the circumstances…'

She already knew what he was going to say but it still came as a shock.

'You could always stay here.'

'Well, I'm not sure. I wouldn't want to put you out…'

'You wouldn't be. I'll make up a bed on the sofa,' he said hastily. 'In the morning, we could get some of the induction out of the way so you can hit the ground running when you start next Monday.'

Beth felt fate had taken a particularly cruel twist of late. 'It does sound like a practical solution,' she said, trying desperately to make the arrangement seem like a sound business proposition. 'But I don't like to put you out. Maybe I should head for the station…'

He raised his eyebrows.

'You're right. Bad idea. Sleeping at Euston. Can I borrow your phone to ring home? They'll be worried that I might be caught up in the travel chaos—or worse, knowing dad.'

'The phone's on my desk in the study.'

Beth thought it best to tell her father she was staying in a hotel at the company's expense rather than explain how she'd ended up in her new boss's apartment. She also asked him to tell Marcus she'd been delayed, and then turned off her mobile, in case he called. The thought of being forced to pretend she was in a hotel in front of Jack made her blood run cold. When she walked back into the sitting room, the smell of coffee and the burbling of an espresso machine was drifting in from the kitchen.

'Do you want a drink and something to eat?' called Jack.

'Yes. Yes, please.' She hovered halfway to the sofa. It was bizarre, this polite conversation. It was like she'd come to tea with an old acquaintance she hadn't seen for years. Jack emerged from behind the counter, wearing battered old combats and clutching a T-shirt she assumed he'd just pulled from the washing machine. He stretched up his arms to pull it on. Her eyes were drawn to his abs; as he reached up, they tightened, leaving a provocative hollow. The waistband of his trousers parted a little from his stomach. No way was he an acquaintance, old or otherwise.

'Make yourself at home. I'll get us something to eat,' he said, then quickly, as if he'd felt the irony as sharply as she had, he turned away.

His idea of food turned out to be a packet of Mars bars, tortilla chips, and a jar of salsa. Plus coffee and two glasses with what looked like brandy.

'It's not hemlock or anything mind-bending,' he said, catching her wary expression. 'Just a coffee and a drop of Armagnac. You look like you need it.'

'Maybe I do,' she said, accepting the glass and a chocolate bar.

She didn't really want more alcohol. Bawling like a girl, a restless night, and alcohol on an empty stomach had finally caught up with her and given her a killer headache. Luckily she'd found some pills at the bottom of her bag and popped three while she was in Jack's study. They seemed to have started working and by the time she'd finished her Mars bar, Jack had got down half his brandy.

'Are you OK?' he asked as she massaged her forehead.

'Fine… I did have a bit of a headache, but that's going off.'

He poured himself another drink. Beth dipped a tortilla in the salsa and cast her eyes around the room.

'This is some apartment. Very trendy and minimalist. Must have cost you a bit.'

He chose an armchair opposite her. 'I'm only renting it temporarily, but you're right, it's not half bad. Just right for a bloke on his own, definitely.'

She'd already noticed the lack of feminine touches in the flat. Then again, there could always be a pink toothbrush in the bathroom or a lacy thong stuffed down the sofa. Just because he didn't actually have a live-in partner, didn't mean there wasn't someone willing to curl up on the leather sofa with him or share a stir-fry in his kitchen.

She raised her glass in the direction of the windows. 'It's a spectacular view. Really amazing.'

'Like I said, it's perfect for one. I've got all the bars and restaurants I can handle on the doorstep—not to mention the fact that it's a short walk from the office, which is a huge bonus—it means I can work even longer hours.'

'How did you find it? Did the company help you?'

'They arranged everything as part of the relocation package and I figured it was a good idea to take it. I guess I'll have to buy something soon or I'll be out of the property market for good. That's what everyone keeps telling me. So I suppose it's a good job I kept my old place in Windsor and rented it out. There's a tenant there now and, besides, it's too far to commute.'

'How long were you in the U.S.?' she asked, beginning to think she might get through the evening after all. 'Awhile, I guess? Long enough to get a transatlantic twang.'

'Is it that obvious?'

'Only a little. I don't expect it's terminal.'

He grinned, the kind of boyish grin that, she recalled, had got her into trouble in the first place. Then he swirled the brandy round in his glass. 'To answer your question, I'd been over there about five years—maybe a bit more. I started as Operations Manager then worked my way up to being Vice President.'

'That sounds impressive.'

He pulled a face. 'Oh God, no—the title's much grander

than it sounds. But Big Outdoors were obviously fooled, so they headhunted me. I've been over here awhile but nothing was made official which is why,' he added carefully, 'you didn't know I was at the helm.'

She was telling herself not to be fooled by his self-deprecation. He must have climbed the ladder pretty fast to end up as a CEO this quickly.

'You're the boss. You're entitled to recruit in whatever way you want, as long as it's legal. You could say,' she murmured, returning his gaze at last, 'that you wanted to see how I handled the unexpected.'

'I guess I deserved that,' he replied, pouring more coffee and keeping his eyes on her in a way that made her shift a little in her seat. The leather squeaked as she moved. He took a swift gulp of his brandy. She matched him and coughed as a trail of fire flowed down her throat.

'Sorry, it's the real McCoy, just a bit in-your-face,' he said.

'You can say that again.'

They both laughed out loud and she noticed that her head had stopped throbbing. She wrinkled her toes and realized just why it felt so nice. She'd kicked off her shoes and had her feet stretched out under Jack's table.

An hour later, or maybe it was two, Beth found herself lying full-length on the black sofa. She was stuffed with

72

tortilla chips, her lips were tingling with chili salsa, and the neck of the Armagnac bottle was clutched between her fingers.

'Beth. It's getting late.'

Her eyes focused slowly. Jack—she was pretty certain it was him—was standing next to her and, for some reason, was trying to steal a bottle from her. Why he was there at all was a mystery to her. It had been such a long time… ah… she began to recall. He'd given her a job. She clutched at the bottle again, but he prised it from her fingertips.

'Let me have this. You've had enough,' he said.

'Don't be a spoilsport. One little drink won't hurt me.'

'It will on top of these,' he said, holding up a white packet. 'They fell out of your bag. These are prescription painkillers. Your dad's name is on the label. How many have you had?'

'One or two… maybe three in the bar. Anothercouple laterIdunno.'

Loosening her fingers from the bottle, he shook his head at her double-glazed eyes. 'Try and sit up. I'll get you a glass of water.'

'Oh Jack, the night is young… don't be such a boring old fart.'

'I'd better get you into bed,' he said sternly, then regretted it.

'Woo-hooo. Aren't you strict?' she giggled. 'I'm a big

73

girl now, Jack Thornfield. I don't need you to tell me what to do.'

'Be quiet and let me help you up,' he said gruffly.

Jack was totally pissed off with himself—if he was honest, a bit pissed per se. When he'd offered Beth a brandy, he'd only wanted her to relax, not to get her drunk as a skunk. She'd seemed fine and she'd only had two glasses—but then again, he'd had to go into his study to take a call at one point. He'd only been away about ten minutes but the bottle did look suspiciously low. Maybe she'd been topping up the glass or, more likely, his judgment was distinctly on the hazy side.

She held out her hand and, as he went to take it, pulled him down suddenly. He was a big man but she caught him by surprise and he couldn't help collapsing on top of her.

'Oof...'

'Jeez!'

'Jack...'

He was going to ask her if she was all right, but there was no need. Her arms were round his neck, her face was next to his, her lips were an inch away, smelling of Armagnac and chili. It was a strange but enticing combination. Raising her head a fraction, she lifted her mouth to his. He let her open lips rest on his closed ones, tasting for a moment, the salt of tortillas. At that moment, he had the urge to lick every salty grain from her full lips, then taste the rest of her. Instead, he jerked his head back and struggled to disentangle her arms as gently as he could. What the hell had possessed him to offer her a drink in the first place? Oh yes, he remembered: he'd wanted to be nice to her. Nice one, Jack.

'Get up, please.'

Her arm hung limply over the edge of the sofa, her eyes stared at him and a small, slightly deranged smile tilted the corners of her mouth.

'Mmm… you know what, Jack… boss… I don't think I can.'

'Stop calling me that.'

'OK, boss.'

'Shit.'

'Whadidyousay…'

He couldn't reply because he was grunting with the effort of hoisting her up off the sofa and into his arms. His thighs protested and his biceps quivered as he straightened up. It wasn't like in the movies; she wasn't a stick-insect and he was tired. She was also completely out of her tree. The irony was not lost on him. How many times in the past had he fantasized about having Beth spend the night in his apartment? Except this wasn't Beth, was it? Not really. This Beth absolutely couldn't stand him and was only here because she was desperate, drugged, and drunk—the latter being his fault.

'I know your type,' she slurred, clinging to his neck and bringing her face up close to his as he staggered towards the bedroom. 'I know you—you'll have my knickers off before I can say Kilijanmaro.'

'You're totally safe with me, I can promise you that. And by the way, it's Kili*man*jaro.'

The sober Beth he'd once known would have socked him one by now. The wriggling vamp in his arms let out a shriek of mirth. He winced as his eardrums throbbed.

'Ooohhh… get you…'

He managed to open the door to his bedroom with his back, as Beth giggled in his arms. 'This shuit is a pain in the bum. The skirt's too tight and I nearly couldn't get my leg over a bloke's parcel on the Tube. He was sooooo hairy and he reeked of garlic.'

'Really?' he said, laughing, because if he didn't laugh he'd be crying in frustration at having a half-dressed Beth, willing and up for it, in his bedroom and not being able to do a thing about it.

'And this blouse,' she said, looking straight down her cleavage. 'It's wayyyy too hot in your sanctum, you know—or is it too cold? Whatever, I hate that air-conditioning. It's not environmentally friendly you know. It's an insult to the ozone layer. I should report you to the energy com—commis—the authortish.'

My God, he thought, she was outrageous when she was drunk. God knows what she'd be like in the morning.

'I've already been reported to every commission on the planet,' he said, plonking her down on the purple suede throw. 'And you've had far too much brandy. I'm putting you to bed.'

As she allowed him to unwind her arms from his neck, Beth reached for a furry cushion and hugged it. Drowsed with alcohol and exhaustion, she tried to concentrate on him. He seemed to be reaching up into a gaping black mouth which morphed into a walk-in wardrobe. As he came sharply into focus, her eyes were fixed on the combat trousers tautening across his backside. Maybe if she reached out she could grab a hold of him...

, Her fingers clutched the air.

'Jack,' she mumbled, turning onto her stomach as her world swirled, 'did anyone ever tell you have the most fantastic arse?'

His retreating voice drifted into her fuzzy brain as she began to drool into the pillow.

'Go to sleep. For my sake if not yours.'

Later, Jack lay in his boxers on the leather sofa, slithering around under his winter trench coat. As he'd pulled it out of his wardrobe he hadn't been able to help staring at Beth, cosseted under his duvet. In rest, he could see she looked older but only in a good way. There was depth and character in her still-delicate features and he liked the way her honey-blond hair spread over the pillow, making him want to thread his fingers through it.

He was almost glad the sofa was so uncomfortable—so un-bed-like. He needed the twenty-first century equivalent of a hair shirt to take his mind off what he'd seen when he'd gone into her room to fetch his coat.

She'd thrown the cover and her clothes on the floor, where they lay in a tangled heap. She'd been lying face-down on his bed in only her underwear. She had a deep blue lacy bra and matching thong on, and he had tried his hardest not to remember any more details. Like the little butterfly tattoo on her left cheek that he knew damn well hadn't been there eight years ago. He felt guilty at even seeing it. Even guiltier that he'd taken a step or two across the room to take a closer look.

Now the design was etched on his mind: a tiny pink and purple butterfly whose wings fluttered forever in the sweet spot where the curve of her bottom met the small of her back. His hand had hovered inches above it for a moment until she'd stirred slightly in her sleep and hugged her legs tighter to her chest. She was cold—and he was a pervert for looking.

Scooping up the cover from the floor, he laid it gently over her body, then walked out of his bedroom, closing the door on her as carefully as he could. He knew damn well that letting Beth get drunk and spend the night in his apartment was a sleazy and highly unprofessional thing to do—hell, she could probably have him sacked for it, whether the contracts were signed or not. But that wasn't what bothered him. It was the fact he'd made her vulnerable again.

When he'd finally given up on sleeping, he got up, made himself a drink, and pulled a letter and a photograph out of the kitchen drawer. He scanned again the formal black typescript on white heavy bond paper. It was all there in black and white, the end of his marriage:

> *Dear Mr. Thornfield, we are writing to inform you that your decree nisi has been pronounced…*

He read on through the legalese again then added his own twist: *… he was officially a statistic. A failed relationship. No longer a husband or a father… Not that he ever had been.*

He felt his guts tighten and the letter fell from his fingers onto the wooden floor. He picked up the photograph of a little boy and ran his fingers over it. The boy had dark hair like his and Jack's insides twisted tighter. He knew he was torturing himself by even looking at Calum now. He knew he'd never see the boy again. He knew he should be relieved that he was free. That his life, from being hopelessly complicated, was no longer entangled with a wife and child.

But he didn't feel free at all. He felt numb and robbed of all that he—and Beth—might have had.

CHAPTER 9

BETH SQUINTED AS SUNLIGHT FILTERED INTO THE STRANGE room and slanted across the big divan she was lying on. For a second, she had been convinced she was back in the 'granny' flat perched above her dad's bike business and that the door she glimpsed out of the corner of a sticky eye led to a little hall, a tiny kitchenette, a one-woman shower room, and a 'cozy' sitting room. She'd slept in so many places in her time. Dossing in a tent, on a scuzzy train, in a dodgy hostel—that didn't bother her. Waking up in Jack Thornfield's bed did.

In fact, she was lying, virtually naked, on his king-size divan under his purple velvet cover.

'Oh, shit!'

Ow. She laid a hand on her forehead. Expletives hurt too much. Thinking hurt too much. The light that was filtering between the white Venetian blinds was making everything painfully clear. She had got drunk, blindingly, toe-curlingly drunk, in her new boss's apartment and he had put her to bed.

She lay back on the pillow. Turning her head to one side, she noticed her suitcase sitting, accusingly, by a chair. Thrown over the seat of the chair were her blouse, skirt, and jacket. Her stomach swished dangerously. Jack must have undressed her because she definitely didn't remember getting undressed.

And what on earth had she said last night? Oh God, what had she done? What if she'd… no, she wouldn't have. He wouldn't have taken advantage of her like that. Surely not—though it hadn't stopped him before.

Grabbing her clothes from the chair, she scuttled into the shower room and locked the door. The creature from the black lagoon stared back at her from the mirror. Clumps of day-old mascara clogged her lashes and streaked the dark circles under her eyes. Her hair, always unwilling to submit, had defied gravity and stuck up on one side only, giving her a crest like the cockerel in their neighbor's garden. Her face matched the white tiles and she vowed never ever to touch alcohol again. At least, she consoled herself, as she turned on the shower controls, Marcus would never find out.

———

In the kitchen, Jack heard the distant whoosh of the shower and cursed himself again. He was sitting at the breakfast bar, toying with a slice of toast and wondering just when he'd be hauled up before the board and sacked for inviting an employee into his apartment. Or when Beth would sue him for sexual harassment. Jeez, she had every right to sue him, no matter what his intentions had been. At the end of the day, his new employee had ended up in his bed, half naked. She could claim he'd done almost anything to her while she was under the influence.

Some time later as he refilled the coffee machine, he heard heels tapping on the wooden floor. Beth was standing there, looking a bit fragile and very pale. Her downcast face told him she'd rather be at the bottom of the sea than within fifty feet of him.

'Morning,' he said gruffly, as she lingered in the sitting area. 'Do you want a coffee?'

'Could I just have tea, please?'

'Sure you can. Toast?'

She climbed onto a stool at the far end of the breakfast bar. 'No thanks.'

He plonked a tea bag in a mug, poured hot water on top of it, then reached for a carton from the fridge. 'Milk?'

She nodded her head and he could see the wince from the other side of the kitchen.

He handed her the mug.

'Thanks,' she murmured, keeping her eyes on the tea. Her hair was damp and fluffed around her head like a blond halo.

'You got the shower working, then?' he said.

'Um… after a fashion.'

'Good. That's… very good.'

'Yes. Um… do you have any sugar?'

'Sure,' said Jack, sliding a packet over the granite countertop.

As Jack shoved the milk back in the fridge, Beth was wishing for a hole to open up in the floor and swallow her down. She was still angry with him, still hurt at what had happened, and there was also another, stronger feeling: fear. What if she had, actually, slept with him? Imagine how many times more excruciating this morning would be? She watched him push a crust of toast around his plate and swallowed hard as he caught her looking at him.

'Beth, I know I shouldn't be saying this…'

Her stomach churned.

'I shouldn't even be thinking it, but when your résumé dropped onto my desk, I thought, maybe, that us meeting like this—as colleagues of course—was fate…'

As he spoke the words, half awkward, half wistful, a wave of panic washed over her. If she had slept with Jack, her position this morning would be impossible rather than just excruciating. She might have destroyed the new job she had fought so hard for, and she'd have betrayed Marcus. He was a good man and he certainly didn't deserve that kind of treatment—especially not with the likes of Jack. The lines had to be drawn even more clearly between them; thick, indelible lines that neither of them would ever dare cross.

Her heart beat out a tattoo as she spoke. 'You know what? I'm one of those people who doesn't, actually, believe in fate. I applied for the job, you needed someone. It's just a coincidence. Despite what we may like to think, this is a very small world and our paths were bound to cross sometime. I mean,' she said, placing her mug on the countertop and smiling a smile she didn't feel one bit, 'come on. It's not really fate, is it, how we meet our future partner? It just… kind of happens. No one up there is waiting with a bow and arrow aimed at our hearts. People meet in a practical way through friends and at work—like we have now. It doesn't mean it's been ordained in the stars or anything.'

He seemed startled. 'I'm not sure what you mean.'

'You see,' she continued, trying to avoid his eyes, 'no one shot an arrow at me and my partner. It wasn't thunderbolt city or anything. We just happened to live in the same village, we liked each other, and we got together. Nothing fateful about it; it just happened naturally.'

'Your partner?'

'Yes.'

'So it's serious, is it? With you and him?'

'We're practically engaged,' she murmured.

'Who is he?'

'Does it really matter?'

'I'd like to know.'

She shook her head, feeling goose bumps pricking her skin. 'I'm sure you don't want every gory detail of my love life,' she said, smiling in what she hoped was a casual, light-hearted way.

'Gory? That's a funny way of describing your future husband.'

'You know what I meant…'

'Surely there can be no harm in telling me his name?' he said, smiling but also folding his arms across his chest. His jaw tightened.

'Does it really matter?'

'Well, I have no right to pry, of course. But hey, at least tell me his name. I'm bound to be hearing about him in the office if you're going to get married. I might even be asked to add to the collection… maybe get an invite to the evening do…'

'I said we were almost engaged.'

'*Almost?*'

A pulse beat in her temple. 'Well, there's no date fixed yet but I've—known him a long time.'

'Then you can tell me who he is?'

She looked away from him over the Ansel Adams print and took a deep breath. 'It's Marcus. Marcus Frayle.'

Jack was used to surprises. You didn't get where he was without being able to cope with the unexpected. But the idea that Beth could be getting married to another man had dealt him a body blow. Yet he also knew he had no right to be shocked. How could he have assumed she hadn't got someone else? After all these years? Now he came to think of it, it was ludicrous to think she *wouldn't* have been pursued by lots of other men.

'What will Marcus think of you spending the night with me in my apartment?' he said softly, not adding that she'd been practically begging him to make love to her. The vision of her lying, half naked, in his bed turned him on even now.

'He won't be angry. Why should he be? I mean, we haven't done anything wrong, have we? We couldn't help what happened with the bomb scare and the hotels—not that he needs to know. No one needs to know I stayed here. Do they, Jack?'

'No, of course not. We've done nothing wrong. Nothing at all.'

Thrusting his mobile phone into his trouser pocket, he headed for the bedroom. 'I need to get my laptop,' he said, knowing he looked calm, because he could see himself in the polished chrome of the fridge. But, like his reflection, he felt distorted and strange and not quite real. He'd lost her again, let her slip away, even though he'd never really come close to having her in the first place.

He raised his coffee mug to her. 'Well, congratulations to you and Marcus. I hope you'll both be very happy,' he said. 'Now, do you mind very much if we get to work?'

CHAPTER 10

IT WAS LATE WHEN BETH FINALLY GOT HOME TO THE Lakes. The last of the daffodils were still out in a tub by the door and the April evening was raw rather than mild like in London.

'Hello, love,' said her dad, opening the door and kissing her cheek, as she reached the front door of the shop.

'Dad, you shouldn't have got up to come to the door. I've got my key.'

'No trouble. You look a bit rough, love.'

'Well, thanks, Dad!' she said, raising her eyebrows. Actually, she thought, he had a point. She'd seen herself in the loo on the train and reckoned she could give Shrek a run for his money in the green-stakes.

'You've been OK without me, I see,' she said, catching sight of a vase of fresh flowers on the kitchen windowsill. There was no pile of washing up in the sink, and by the sparkling windows, it seemed as if the cleaning fairy had dropped by. A fairy by the name of Honor, if she wasn't mistaken.

'Louisa's out. She left you a card,' said her dad as she flopped down on a chair. The card was propped up on the kitchen table against a milk carton, stuffed in a pink envelope bearing her name in Louisa's bold handwriting. She tore open the envelope and grinned.

'It's a congratulations card,' she said, sliding it over the kitchen table to him.

'Do you want anything to eat?'

'No… no, I'm fine. I might just get straight off and have a bath, if you don't mind. You are pleased I got the job, aren't you?' she asked as he read the card.

'Of course I am.'

'Are you sure? I haven't upset you, have I, by going to London?'

He finally met her eye and lifted his chin. 'I'm proud of you, Beth. You and Louisa both, but I wish you hadn't had to do it. It should be me supporting the family.'

Her heart sank a little. 'Please don't say that. You can't help what's happened and it makes me proud to be able to help. If I can't look after my own family when the chips are down, who can?'

She wound her arms around his shoulders and hugged him 'Dad, I love you. You and Lou-lou. And we'll stick together just like we always have, no matter what happens.'

She felt the pressure of his hand against her back as they held each other, fighting back the tears. He tightened her grip before they both broke away.

'Where has Lou gone this time?' she asked.

'To a party at the boat club. I warned her to be back by twelve. I don't like the lot that go down there. Always smoking wacky tobacky and knocking back cheap cider like it's going out of fashion. Honor says I'm worrying too much, but I can't help it. And as for that Greg Wilson, he's a total waster.'

'Hmm. He's trouble, but I shouldn't worry about the booze,' she added, thinking of her own performance the previous night last night and crossing her fingers. 'Or about Greg. Louisa's got her head screwed on.'

'I'm still going to wait up,' he said firmly.

'It could be late, Dad.'

'All the same…'

Knowing when to admit defeat with him, she changed the subject. 'Louisa said Marcus had been round while I was away…'

'He has. He was fishing for some info on the local council. Fancies getting into politics, I think. I don't think I told him anything very useful…' he paused, then added, 'He asked after you.'

'What did you tell him?'

'I said you'd got another interview yesterday. I thought there was no point in going into it all before we knew you'd got the job.'

'I've spoken to him once and I'm going to tell him everything tomorrow.'

'How do you think he'll take it?'

'I don't know. I can still see him, you know. He can come and visit me and I'll be home as often as I can. It's not the other side of the world…'

But it almost was, as far as Marcus was concerned. The next morning, she caught him during a lunch break at the Frayle dealership. They sat on a bench behind the showroom and ate Cumbrian sausage on rolls overlooking the lake.

'I know it's a shock but I have to do this,' said Beth, throwing a piece of roll to the ducks crowding greedily round their bench.

'Don't do that. It only encourages them to come onto the premises,' said Marcus, eyeing a mallard with distaste.

Beth reached for his hand and squeezed it. 'Marcus, I'm sorry I didn't tell you about the job but it all happened so fast. I didn't even expect to get a reply, let alone an interview, and as for landing this job—'

'How long will you be away?'

She hesitated, just long enough.

'That bad?'

She sighed. 'Six months.'

'Doing what, may I ask?'

'Product Manager, responsible for the development of the European program. It's a temporary role, almost a consultancy job, so the money's good and it will be great on my résumé. They're called Big Outdoors—you might have heard of them…'

'Actually, no, I haven't,' said Marcus, eyeing her critically from his cool blue eyes. He *was* very good-looking, especially today in his Armani suit and pale blue shirt. Lots of women for miles were after him. She was lucky to have a man like him who cared about her. If their relationship could survive six months and three hundred miles of on-off separation, then surely it *must* be the real thing.

'You may as well know I'm not happy about you going off like this,' he said cutting into her thoughts. 'You might have told me first; instead I had to hear it off Louisa.'

'That was very wrong of me but I didn't want to mention it until I was sure it was all definite. It was a long shot, really, but in hindsight, I agree that it wasn't fair on you.'

'No, it wasn't,' he said, shaking his foot at a duck.

'But six months isn't that long and it's only London. I'll be back home as often as I can and you can come down and see me if you can get away from work. We can have lots of fun.'

He looked thoughtful and then his face brightened. 'Well, I'm no fan of London, as you know. That bloody congestion charge is a crackpot notion for a start, but you do have a point. If I can get Robert Haynes to take over here for a weekend, I could give the Porsche a good blast down the outside lane of the M6. I've been meaning to see how the old girl performs on a long run—and see you, of course,' he added.

'Yes,' she said, relieved to see him happier again. She slipped her arm through his. 'You see, it really isn't the end of the world, after all, and Camden Town is on the edge of the charging zone so you won't have to fork out.'

'It's not the money, it's the principle,' said Marcus, pursing his lips.

They finished their lunch while she told him more about the job and listened to his plans to run for the local council. Then, hand-in-hand, they started to walk back up the grass towards the showroom.

'Shit!'

Marcus lifted up his foot and wrinkled his nose.

'What's up?' she asked.

'Those bloody ducks will have to go. These shoes cost nearly two hundred quid!'

CHAPTER 11

JACK LOOSENED HIS TIE AND UNDID HIS TOP BUTTON AS the August sun beat down fiercely on the plate-glass windows. Even with the air-con up high, his office was stuffy as the temperature reached the eighties out on the London streets.

It seemed a long, long time since Beth had slunk out of his apartment the day following her interview. In the months that had passed since then, he'd done his utmost not to treat her as anything more than a colleague. And he'd succeeded. Most of the time.

In fact, there had been occasions over the past few months when he hadn't seen her for days on end. She'd been abroad quite a bit, liaising with suppliers, assessing and setting up tours. He'd been away too, at a series of industry conferences.

It was when they were both in the office that the trouble started. Only the previous week, he'd been hearing her present at one of the fortnightly product managers meetings. It had taken every ounce of his concentration to focus on her report and not the sassy skirt and heels she was wearing. Or rather, what was in them.

He picked up the desk phone, determined to focus on his work. 'Martha, are you still here?'

'It seems that way, Jack. What can I do for you?' Martha sounded as world-weary as ever.

'Before you leave, could you just drop an email to Freya Scott? I need to reschedule our discussion of her promotion.'

'No problem. But you know, you don't really have to do that. One of the HR people could take care of it for you.'

'I'd like to have a one-to-one with as many staff as possible as soon as possible. It will help me get to know the team better,' he said firmly, aware that another one-to-one with him might be as welcome as colonic irrigation.

'It's done. I'll arrange a time with Freya.'

'Thanks. Now get off home.'

Drafting in Freya to help Beth develop the European portfolio had been a great idea and now she deserved an official promotion to Assistant Product Manager. Freya was enthusiastic and keen to learn and Beth seemed to be thriving on the responsibility. They get on well together out of the office too. He'd seen them together in the Fat Face store in Covent Garden a couple of weeks before. Not that he went clothes shopping that often, but he'd 'needed' some new jeans for dress-down Fridays. He hoped they hadn't noticed him coming out of the changing rooms laden with a surfer sweatshirt and three T-shirts as well as the jeans. The phone rang, startling him. It was Martha again.

'Oh, I almost forgot—that travel journalist woman called back,' she said.

'Camilla Reed?'

'Yes. That's the one. I said you were in a meeting and that I'd pass on the message. She's insisting you call her.'

He could almost hear his PA's knowing smile down the line. Camilla calling him regularly, now that *would* give Martha something to think about.

'OK. I'll see if I can get hold of her now. Have a nice evening, Martha.'

He opened his BlackBerry and found Camilla's number. From what he could remember of her from the States, she was willowy, blonde, and every inch as uptown as her perfectly formed vowels. He suspected an in-depth profile wasn't the only thing she was interested in but had decided that might not be such a bad thing. Mightn't a little bad behavior with Camilla be just what he needed right now? Beth was happily coupled up, why shouldn't he have a bit of fun? He wasn't a monk, after all...

The ringtone had barely had time to squeak before she picked it up.

'Why hello, Jack. I thought you'd left the country or been kidnapped by aliens,' she said coolly.

He shook his head, a smile on his face. 'Nope. Just mega busy with work. Sorry I haven't got back to you sooner.'

'Poor you. Working your bottom off keeping the peasants in line.'

'The guys have been working very hard. They keep *me* in line, as a matter of fact. We're in the middle of a major expansion, as you may know from the trade press.'

He heard her tutting on the end of the line. 'Jack, darling, *relax*. I get the corporate message loud and clear. Now, I presume because you've finally deigned to call, that you're going to concede defeat and grant me my interview.'

'I suppose I'll have to surrender, won't I?'

'I'm afraid you will. Now, let me see when I can fit you in. Hmm, I'm in Switzerland for a few days but I'm free after that. You can pick me up on Friday at seven. Number 223, West Court, Knightsbridge.'

'I'll have to check my calendar first…'

'I *don't* think so,' she snapped. 'You see, I've been checking up on you and I doubt you've any other offers. You're a workaholic. Everyone in the business says so. I absolutely won't take no for an answer so there's no escape. Be there at seven or I might have to get very cross indeed,' she added sharply.

The following Friday, Beth found herself on her hands and knees in the dark. She was rummaging frantically in the stationery cupboard in the office she shared with Freya. Knowing she had precisely five minutes to find the paper, print off her latest progress report, and collate it ready for the product managers' meeting.

'Freya! Do you know where the printer paper is? It's run out again!'

She lifted up a pile of Christmas decorations in the recesses of the cupboard, hoping a miracle would unearth a forgotten ream of paper underneath the tinsel. She'd spent until the last minute polishing the report to perfection. She'd had to. Jack had been pushing all the managers really hard over the past few months. He expected them to come up with new revenue-producing tours and was constantly setting new targets. He also expected everyone at her level to meet up with him every two weeks and brief him of new and existing work. Today, she was presenting with Tom Jeffries, the South American product manager and Shreeya Patel, who developed the African sector.

'Freya, hon!' she called, as the stationery cupboard drew a blank. 'Do you know where the paper is? I'd hate to be late for this, not after all the work we've both put in on these new tour ideas.'

'Here we are. Chill.'

'You are a complete star,' said Beth, straightening up to find Freya bearing a ream of paper. 'Where d'you get it?'

'That skinny surfer dude in the accounts department.'

'Ohh. What did you have to do for it?'

'Sell my body,' said Freya, hiding the rest of the paper in her drawer.

'That goes beyond the call of duty,' said Beth as the printer decided to play ball for once.

'We-ell... I did have to promise to go tubing at the Snodome.'

'Freya, you are a star and I just don't know what—'

'You'd do without me?'

'Not spend so much money on clothes? Drink within the recommended limits? Not be trying out Goji berries and pomegranate juice and any other craze that's going to be the key to eternal life and a state of earthly bliss?'

Freya pushed out her tongue. 'Don't mock. Goji berries are good. Dave brought some back from the Himalayas. They have five hundred times the Vitamin C of oranges and the locals say people who eat them have a life expectancy of one hundred and fifty.'

'I'll have a life expectancy of five minutes if I don't get this printed off for the meeting. And by the way, I couldn't have got through the past few months without you.'

'Shall I collate the report for you?'

'Yes, please. And do you have stats and demographics on the Lapland trekking package?'

Freya tapped a folder on her desk. 'Right here.'

'You're a geek. You know that?'

Freya pulled a face. 'No one's ever called me a geek before, but I suppose I could get used to it. Now get a move on or you'll be late for He Who Must Be Obeyed.'

Beth smiled in what she hoped was an enigmatic way,

then, clutching the folder, she dashed out of the office towards the management suite.

As she walked inside, Tom and Shreeya were already sitting around the mini-boardroom table. Their boss, however, was nowhere to be seen.

'Where's Jack?'

'Bathroom?' offered Tom Jeffries.

'Batcave?' said Shreeya Patel.

'Boardroom,' said Jack, from behind them. 'I've just been on the phone to the chairman and I've told him you're all about to make my day with your stunning sales figures and inspired new product ideas.'

Laughter, soft and expected, filled the room. Beth's stomach fluttered gently. It was dress-down Friday. Jack's suit hung on a hanger from the coat stand in the corner. Just in case he had to meet anyone important, she thought, but for now, he was wearing a Fat Face T-shirt. Spread across his broad chest was a slogan that read: *'Better a bad day on the water than a good one in the office.'* She stifled a laugh as he ordered coffees and Danish from Martha. She was sure these were the clothes she and Freya had spotted him buying a few weeks ago.

'OK, joking apart,' he said, pulling out a chair, 'I know you're all working flat out, but I think these meetings are really valuable. We've made significant progress already and some of your new tours are now on the website and selling, but we can't let up, not even for a moment. Tom, do you want to kick off?'

Beth tried to concentrate on her colleagues' reports as Jack occasionally nodded in approval then followed it up with a barrage of questions. As Shreeya was finishing her presentation, the door opened and Martha came in with the coffee and pastries.

'Let's have five minutes,' said Jack.

She nibbled at a pain au chocolat, but inside her stomach swirled. She didn't know why these meetings had such an effect on her. She'd done her homework and she had some great ideas to present. If only she didn't keep getting fixated on Jack's arms. He had an Animal watch on today and the Velcro was strapped a little too tightly round his wrist.

'Beth? Are you ready?'

'Um?'

'The European report?'

She desperately hoped she wasn't blushing. 'Oh, sorry. Yes. Europe.'

Quickly, she gathered herself and launched into her presentation, running through the new tour ideas she and Freya had come up with and costed out.

'Interesting,' said Jack, when she'd finished. 'Some promising ideas there.'

Promising, she thought, promising sounded good. Possibly.

'I really buy into the mountain bike package and

as for the idea of Turkish white-water rafting on the Coru—inspired.'

She tried to stop herself breaking into a grin. 'I tried the rafting myself a few years ago. It was awesome. But what do you think about the dog sledding break?'

Jack paused, flicking through the report. 'An interesting idea—sleeping in genuine Sami tents, looking after your own husky team, then visiting ICEHOTEL in Jukkasjarvi…'

'Profitable too,' she added.

'The figures look like they have potential…'

'But?'

'Not a but. Not really. On the other hand, you know, I think we could get even more of a margin out of these figures. And I'm not sure you've got a broad enough demographic. Not quite. Can you have a rethink and report back later today?'

'Today?'

'Yes, please. I have a meeting with the board on Monday. I'd like to go and present this as something on the website, knowing the figures are cut-and-dried.'

'Well, I'll do my best, but I'm not sure whether there's much room for maneuver from the supplier and we don't want to compromise the quality of the experience.'

Jack smiled. 'Convince them of the attractiveness of gaining a foothold in our business. Don't be afraid of a bit of brinkmanship. Let me know what you come up with. I'll be around until eight-ish.'

'So,' said Tom, as the managers walked out of the meeting later. 'No Friday sushi this lunchtime?'

'And I presume you won't make the film after work?' said Shreeya, pulling a face.

Beth sighed. 'It does look like I'll have to pass on the sushi but I'll do my best to get to the film, if I can have these revamped stats ready. I'll see you there or meet you in the Bird in Hand afterwards.'

It was almost 7 p.m. when she found herself knocking on Jack's office door. He was still sitting at his desk, writing.

'Um… hi,' she said, suddenly feeling shy at being alone with him so late. 'I've brought the updated husky report. I've emailed you a copy too, but I wanted to bring these competitor brochures in to see what you thought of the opposition.'

'Let's have a look,' he said, indicating the table.

She'd had been hoping to leave the brochures and get away as fast as possible, knowing that if she was quick, she might just be able to slip in to the movie after the ads. However, he clearly intended to discuss the package further. She thrust aside the idea of making the start of the movie and spread the brochures on the table.

'Do you want a coffee while we take a look at these?'

Beth hadn't managed a drink since Freya had plonked a raspberry smoothie and a Gillian McKeith bar on her desk at two o'clock. Besides, her throat felt dry.

'Yes, thanks.'

He poured out two mugs of coffee and handed her one. Steam rose from her coffee and she blew it away.

'I've found a way to increase the margin without affecting the quality of the package,' she said, as he studied a competitor mailshot. 'I phoned the supplier and I think they'd be willing to move slightly on their costs.'

'I knew you could do it,' he said, smiling encouragingly.

'And Freya and I have refined the new marketing strategy,' she said, thinking, annoyingly, that his eyes reminded her of a midnight sky. *'They come out at night...'* Freya would have added.

Beth let out a giggle

Jack looked confused and she put her hand over her mouth. 'Sorry, just thinking of something Freya told me.'

His eyes really *were* a gorgeous color, though, she thought as she reverted into serious mode.

'Yes, we've come up with a completely fresh sales strategy,' she said.

'That's great,' Jack went on, pulling a brochure towards him. It showed a Sami camp, the Northern Lights illuminating the sky behind the tents. 'Beth, I know you think I'm pushing you and that's because I am.'

She felt her stomach flutter dangerously. 'It's what you employed me for.'

'True, but I do appreciate the fact that you're prepared to go the extra mile. This Lapland idea is inspired. Do you want some chocolate?' he asked unexpectedly.

'Um... why not?'

Moments later, he'd produced a bar of Green & Black's from his desk drawer and was holding it out to her. The scent of dark orange chocolate wafted temptingly into her nose. She broke off a square and popped it in her mouth, telling herself the warm glow inside was coffee and professional pride, that Jack would have offered praise where it was due to any of the other managers; he wasn't singling her out for any special reason.

He pointed at the photograph on the brochure. 'Imagine being there now, sleeping in the snow, watching the Northern Lights.'

She nodded. 'Yes. It would be something. I saw them in Canada once. Like a fluorescent rainbow taking up the whole sky.'

'I saw them too. Years ago, just after I left university; I was in Troms in Norway and I've never seen anything like it before or since. I think I sat for about an hour watching them and every inch of me was numb when I managed to tear myself away.'

'When I first saw them, I couldn't believe they were real. I mean, I know they're just caused by the sun, but they seemed—it sounds silly—magical. You know, unearthly somehow.'

'I thought they looked like ghostly waterfalls shimmering in the sky,' said Jack quietly.

'Or gigantic veils.'

'You know,' he went on, 'I really envy you your job. I know it's hard work, but getting out of office to actually see these places is something I really miss. I don't get out into the field anywhere near as much as I used to. I miss getting too cold, being uncomfortable, challenged, jolted…'

'…too hot, tired, bored, exhilarated, dead on your feet, but having to smile and have another shot of the local brew even when you'd rather be in your bed,' said Beth wistfully.

'Forgetting your passport…'

'More shots…' She shuddered.

He grimaced. 'I don't miss that bit, but I wouldn't mind a bit of sleeping on trains or on the ground…'

She laughed. 'Huddled in a tent or curled up by the campfire. Warm and cozy while the wind howls outside and the Northern Lights blast the sky.'

He reached for the brochure and brushed against her arm with his. His fingers lingered for a second against her wrist and left it tingling with sensation. Then, quickly, he took the brochure and got to his feet.

'OK. That about wraps it up. Thanks for staying late and I'll see you on Monday. Can I keep this for a while?'

'Yes… sure.' Her heart was racing and she was already wondering if she'd imagined his touch.

'Have a good weekend. Are you seeing Marcus?' he asked, back at his desk now, beginning to stash some papers in his laptop case.

She was taken aback. 'No, I went home the week-end before last but he's coming up next Friday for Tom's gig.'

'Perhaps I'll finally get to meet him then.'

'Yes, you probably will.'

She gathered up the rest of the brochures in her arms, perplexed and anxious now to get out of his office. If there had been a flicker of intimacy between them, she told herself, it definitely had been imagined.

'If it's OK, I'm going to get off. If I go now, I might still make a film I'd like to see with some of the guys.'

Jack barely glanced up at her as she hovered by the door. 'Sure. You get off. Have a good evening.'

Five minutes later she was on the pavement outside the building, frantically texting Freya, hoping she hadn't turned her mobile off yet.

'Hey, Beth!'

She turned to find Shreeya and Freya emerging from the coffee shop next to the office. Freya was still slurping the last drops of a frappuccino. 'And why aren't you two guzzling nachos in the Odeon by now?' she asked, smiling as they hurried towards her.

'We've booked into the next show. We know how much you wanted to see Ewan McGregor get his kit off so we lay in wait for you in Starbucks,' said Shreeya.

'Does he get naked in this one too?' asked Beth, relieved to be back out in the real world.

Freya tossed her empty cup in a bin. 'For most of the film, according to *Time Out*.'

'Oh dear,' said Beth, laughing as they set off for the Tube station. 'That sounds absolutely terrible.'

———

Four floors above them, Jack managed to prise himself from the window, where he'd been staring out across the sky since Beth had left. Grabbing his briefcase, he headed for the door. He'd managed to charm a table at Maggiores in Covent Garden and he knew Camilla would have a hissy fit if he was late.

CHAPTER 12

'SO I'M FINALLY GOING TO SEE THE MYSTERIOUS MARCUS,' teased Freya the following week as she and Beth took a quick break from some mind-numbingly boring statistics. 'Are you really bringing him to Tom's gig next Friday?'

'I might be,' said Beth, watching Freya pin a photo of Josh Holloway to her noticeboard.

'Only might?' asked Freya.

'Worry not. You are *definitely* going to meet him.'

Beth had debated about taking Marcus to an 'office' do, however informal, but she'd decided it would do him good to meet her friends and chill out more. She wasn't sure if Jack was going to the gig. She sincerely hoped not.

'Your bloke looks pretty cute from the photos,' said Freya. 'Very smart. Don't you miss him… at night?'

'He's very busy running his business and I've been away over two weekends, so we haven't had many opportunities to get together like that.'

Freya shook her head firmly. 'What a shame. You've got

that nice old place all to yourself and you don't want to waste a brilliant shag pad. Six months is a long time to go without sex. I think I'd wither up altogether. Still, you can make up for it next weekend.'

'I'll have to tidy up, I suppose,' said Beth, desperate to change the subject. 'The flat is a complete dump, but then again I'm away so much I'm surprised I haven't been burgled. When I am there, I hardly have time to do the laundry, let alone do any cleaning. When I got back from Riga, I found a bottle of milk fermenting in the fridge and some furry Brie that practically crawled out of the door.'

'Shouldn't worry,' said Freya airily. 'I heard on GMTV this morning that we all need to build up a resistance to bacteria.'

Beth felt her new Top Shop skirt tighten round her middle as she leant forward to rub a mark off the computer screen. Her eyes felt a bit gritty too, which she put down to lack of sleep combined with living it way too large.

'I daren't get on the scales, with all the bad stuff I've eaten, and I must have had a year's worth of alcohol in the past few months. It's all very well whizzing round local bars and sights, socializing with clients and suppliers until the small hours, but it's hell for your figure.'

Freya sat down at her desk and started to unzip her handbag. 'My heart bleeds for you. I wish I could get my alcohol limit up on the company's expense.'

'You'd soon get fed up with it,' said Beth, as Freya pulled a mirror from her bag and touched up her lip gloss. 'It's hard work, you know. In fact, I might have to show you just how hard it is. How do you fancy getting a taste of it?'

'Oh. My. God. Do you mean it?'

She broke into a grin. 'Yes. Jack agreed in principle for you to check out the Lapland trip last night.'

'Wooo-hoooo!'

'It's work, Frey,' she said, laughing.

'Yeah, yeah!' said Freya. 'Omigod, Lapland. Me and you and a bunch of huskies in a tent.'

'Well, actually maybe not with me…'

'Oh.'

'I'm only on a six-month contract, remember? Unless I can fit the trip in before I finish, we won't be able to go together. It has to be in the winter and I'm done here in the autumn.'

'Can't you get an extension?' pleaded Freya.

'I doubt it, and even if I could, I need to go back home. I promised Marcus and Dad and Lou-lou. This was never meant to be permanent.' Freya looked so absolutely downcast that Beth felt a lump in her throat. Lately, she always seemed to be leaving someone behind. 'I'll see if we can go before I leave, or if you can come with me on another trip. Promise.'

'I guess He Who Must be Obeyed isn't as bad as I thought if he wants me to go out to test a tour,' said Freya, pouring a paper cup of water into Brad Pott, the office cactus. 'I know he can get a bit heavy, but he never bawls you out or gets hormonal. In fact, he doesn't say much to you at all—I mean, he doesn't even try out his jokes on you… I think he's scared of you, to be honest.'

'Really?' Beth managed a shaky laugh. 'He knows I won't be here long, that's all. Besides, I've heard some of his jokes in the product meetings. They're about as funny as David Brent's from *The Office*.'

'David Brent was never that cute,' said Freya. 'Jack may be a git at times, but he's got a fit arse.'

'I hadn't noticed.'

'I still think he's in awe of you. He always speaks so politely, as if he's scared of upsetting you.' Freya broke off suddenly, peering closely at the cactus. 'Do you think this plant is phallic? Personally I think it's obscene.'

'It is a bit… weird. Cacti do have some funny shapes.' Beth wished Freya would get on with some work or talk business. She didn't want to think of phallic things right now. She had an email from Jack in front of her.

Freya had other ideas. 'I do like the odd bollocking from the boss, though,' she went on, carefully turning Brad's pot towards the light.

'You are joking,' laughed Beth.

'Nope. Don't tell *anyone* this, but I get all tingly sometimes when Jack has to remind me to give him the sales figures. I mean I know he's *quite* old…'

'He'll be thirty-five next month. I heard him telling Tom he was getting on a bit,' Beth added hastily. 'So as you say, he's positively ancient.'

'Well… I wouldn't say ancient, but older men can be really sexy, don't you think? Look at Daniel Craig,' said Freya dreamily. 'And even Jack's not that bad. You know, once he asked me to go to his office and explain why I hadn't done something. I just saw him, sitting behind the desk all serious, and I had this sudden urge to—'

'Freya—watch Brad!'

It was too late. The cactus had toppled off the filing cabinet and smashed onto the floor. Soil and broken terra-cotta littered the carpet tiles.

'Poor Brad,' said Freya, getting down on her hands and knees. 'He's gone all limp.'

'I'll take him home and try and replant him,' said Beth, helping her clear up the mess. 'I'm sure Gill won't mind me borrowing a pot.' When calm was restored, she turned to her computer to find an email, as short and cool as an English summer.

From: Jack Thornfield
To: Elizabeth Allen
Subject: Report—HIGH PRIORITY
Please can I have the stats for the Provençal mountain-bike package ready for Friday's team meeting at 10 a.m.
Jack

P.S. I need a copy on my desk by close of play the day before. Thanks.

So, another late night at the office, she thought with a wry smile. Then again, being treated with strict professionalism by Jack *was* what she wanted. She'd established the ground rules between them from the day she'd accepted the job. She was still in the driving seat, here, even if Jack *was* her boss.

'Do you think that cactus hated me personally?' asked Freya, wincing as she pulled a fine spike from her hand with her eyebrow tweezers while Beth digested her email. Jack chose that moment to open their office door without knocking.

'Shit!' cried Freya, dropping her tweezers in her drawer and pretending to look for a paper clip.

'Hello,' said Jack.

Beth heard a strange squeak coming from Freya's desk.

Jack gave Freya a puzzled frown before turning back to Beth. 'Beth, can you come to my office, please?'

'Does it have to be right now? Only I just wanted to phone a Tuscan supplier before they closed.'

'I have to be in a board meeting in ten minutes. If you can't spare the time now, can you make it later? Say after six?'

'Of course. No problem.'

'Thanks. I appreciate it,' he said, staring at Freya as she snorted into her handkerchief.

Beth picked up the phone. Jack hovered in the doorway for a moment and then said very seriously, 'That sounds like a nasty cold you've got, Freya. I should see the company nurse about it.'

'Don't you dare say anything,' said Beth as he strode off and Freya erupted into fits of laughter. 'And before you ask, I don't feel "all tingly" at being ordered about by him.'

But as she walked towards his office later that evening, she found she was fizzing from head to toe.

'Thanks for sparing the time,' he said as she closed the door. 'I know you're busy, but I want to run some ideas by you.'

'It's OK.'

'Come and look at this.'

He indicated a folder on the table overlooking the window.

'I've had this for a few weeks,' he explained as they sat down together. 'I'm being, let's say, "courted" by an enthusiastic supplier and I want your opinion on taking them on as a potential major addition to our portfolio.'

Beth felt ludicrously flattered that he wanted her input. 'It sounds exciting…'

'Hmm. It's a completely new destination for Big Outdoors. I've called you in because it's in your field of expertise. In fact, you could say you've direct experience of it…' He paused, seeming on edge.

She smiled encouragingly. 'It's not cave diving, is it? Or potholing? Because if it is, I've never tried that one.'

'No, not potholing. Nothing quite like that. It's still an adventure travel operator and they specialize in small group activity tours—camping, canyoning, via ferrata, hiking—all that sort of thing.'

'Via ferrata? That *is* a blast. And canyoning—what a great hook for families.'

'Yes, I know.'

A tiny light glimmered in the back of her mind. 'You say it's a European destination. It must be, if you're asking my opinion,' she went on, feeling tension building in her chest. 'It sounds a great proposition. As if it could have broad appeal, but, you know, you haven't actually said where this company is based.'

'Haven't I?' he said, leafing through the papers.

'No, you haven't,' she said firmly, determined to make him look her in the face.

He finally met her eyes. 'It's in Southern Corsica.'

It took a moment before she realized her mouth had dropped open. The silence seemed to stretch out between them, before she managed to find her tongue. 'Corsica?'

He cleared his throat. 'Yes. The company is called Lorenzelli Tours. I happen to know the owner, Olivier Lorenzelli, from years back. He phoned a few weeks back to say his company's expanding. Not that I'd let our connection influence me, beyond professional courtesy, of course.'

'No, of course not.'

'Naturally, he thinks their new tours will fit perfectly in our portfolio and they do appear on the surface to tick all the boxes, but I wasn't able to be totally objective about this. We do have a personal connection and Olivier has been known to get carried away.'

'Right...'

He went on briskly, almost falling over himself to get the words out. 'They have a very professional set-up. With the beaches, mountains, and activities, it should be a great addition to our program—a very wide appeal. This could be a big revenue opportunity if it comes off and, added to other tour ideas from you and the other product managers, I think we'll be on the way to getting Big Outdoors back where it should be in the market. Beth... is that OK?' he asked when she didn't reply.

'Yes. Yes, of course. If you let me have the details, I'll put together an itinerary and get Freya to research the logistics and cost implications.'

'Fine. Good idea.'

'Is that all for now?' she said, the half-open door of his office more tempting than it had ever been.

'Yes, thanks. Update me when you've done the research.'

Outside in the corridor, she gulped in a huge breath. She thought she had everything sorted. She was giving her relationship with Marcus a chance. Making a success of her job. Now, she only knew she was going back *there* and no matter how hard she tried to deny it, she still felt deeply hurt by what Jack had done to her in Corsica. No amount of professionalism could ever change that.

CHAPTER 13

AT THE END OF THE WEEK, BETH FOUND HERSELF DUMPING her Sainsbury's Local bags on the top step of her flat. She'd worked late every night that week, planning the Corsica trip on top of her usual workload. Now, she also had a visit from Marcus to get ready for.

She allowed herself ten minutes of slobbery, then dragged herself off the sofa to clean up before Marcus arrived. She didn't think it was fair to make him live in a pigsty, especially as the Grange, his own place, was always scarily tidy.

Empty takeaway trays filled the sink, the legacy of a night with Tom, Freya, Shreeya, and a few more of the guys from the office. A half-open carton of milk was festering in the fridge door so she poured it down the sink. After chucking out the trays, she plunged the dirty plates in some hot soapy water and rooted in the airing cupboard for some clean sheets to put on the bed. She reckoned she just had time to shower and change into her skinny jeans and sparkly top before Marcus arrived. She was just putting on some lip gloss when she heard him buzz the door.

'Good journey?' she asked, kissing him as she showed him into the flat. To her great relief, he was wearing jeans and a polo shirt, rather than a shirt and tie.

'Not really,' he said, glancing round at the room with a frown. 'I crawled most of the way and the SatNav decided to go haywire as I got off the M25.'

'How horrible for you,' she soothed as he sprawled on the sofa. 'But you're here now.' Marcus pulled a pair of knickers from behind a cushion and raised his eyebrows.

She grabbed her panties. 'Sorry, I'm behind with the laundry. Would you like a beer?'

'What have you got?' he asked, squinting hard at the ceiling.

'Cobra, Stella, Budvar…'

He wrinkled his nose. 'Any chance of some decent red wine?'

'I bought a nice Shiraz, just in case…'

He sighed. 'Oh, go on then, if you're forcing me.'

As she uncorked the bottle and poured them both a glass, he came up behind her and nuzzled her neck. 'Beth…' he whispered.

'Hmm…'

'Did you know you've got rising damp?'

Later, they were pushing their way through the crowds in the Bird in Hand, heading for the back room where Bluesky were already halfway through the first set. The air smelled of chili con carne and spilled beer. Tom's band was making an enthusiastic attempt at Indie rock covers and weren't *that* bad at all, she thought.

Freya was wiggling along to one of the tracks.

'I'll get these,' mouthed Beth, taking her empty glass from her friend's hand. 'Marcus, would you like a pint?'

'Thanks but no thanks. Not at these prices.'

'This is one of the cheapest places for miles,' put in Freya, helpfully. 'You could pay twice as much in the West End.'

Marcus rolled his eyes. 'Daylight robbery.'

'It is a bit steep compared to home. But it's just for one night and Freya's right, the Bird *is* one of the cheapest places.'

'I'll have a half then,' he said, handing over some bills.

Beth headed for the bar, leaving Freya quizzing him tactfully on fast cars. It took awhile to get to the counter and awhile longer to get noticed by the barman. In the end she had to elbow her way between a couple of rugby-sized blokes and shout out her order.

'A half of London Pride, a vodka and Red Bull, and a Sex on the Beach!' she bellowed for the third time just as the band played a last chord and the music stopped.

'Sorry, love, can you speak up?' asked the barman, grinning as the rugby types burst out laughing. 'I'm a bit deaf.'

'Very funny,' she laughed. 'Just the drinks please—the comedy spot comes later.'

She turned back to the throng of drinkers in the pub, trying not to spill any of the drinks. On the stage, Bluesky was accepting pints from a couple of squealing girls. Freya waved excitedly across the room.

She'd almost made it back when she saw Jack.

He was making his way through the crowd and he wasn't alone. The girl next to him was tall, blonde, and stunning. Even the rather distasteful expression on her face couldn't detract from how pretty she was. Jack had his arm on her back, propelling her towards the bar, smiling and nodding at people from work. Alcohol splashed onto the tray she was carrying as her heart sank. But she squared her shoulders and moved on, reminding herself that Jack had every right to bring someone—a *girlfriend*—to any place he wanted. After all, she was here with Marcus. They had both moved on and that had to be good.

She handed Freya a drink, trying not to glance in Jack's direction. 'Where's Marcus gone? I don't want to abandon him.'

'Over there. I introduced him to Dave Stirling,' said Freya. Beth spotted Marcus's blond head, next to the Big Outdoors' IT manager. Beth knew Dave was building a Caterham kit car so she guessed he and Marcus must be in their element.

'Thanks, Freya. I was worried he wouldn't find anyone to talk to.'

'Oh!'

'What's the matter?'

'The boss has brought someone,' hissed Freya, hardly able to contain herself.

'Has he?'

'You can introduce them to Marcus. I'd love to find out who she is—this is going to be interesting!' Freya pointed to her glass. 'That didn't touch the sides,' she said.

Beth found she'd gulped down nearly half her glass. 'I guess I was just a bit thirsty,' she laughed.

'You're telling me. Sure you don't want a Coke or something?'

'No. It's OK, I'll make the rest of it last.'

'I think they might be coming over. Fancy him bringing a woman. Oh, I wonder what he's like in bed?' said Freya, giggling. 'I wonder if he issues a memo asking her to turn out the light to save energy.'

It was true. Jack did have a quite a reputation for money saving 'initiatives' and had recently sent out a long report detailing ways in which the company could be 'greener' and save money. But as for bed? He didn't spare anything, she knew that.

And now he was here, the blonde girl standing cool and aloof beside him. Beth thought she didn't look too happy to be there whereas Jack had a smile on his face.

'Enjoying the gig?' he asked cheerfully.

'Great,' said Beth, smiling back until her jaw hurt.

'It's fab,' trilled Freya excitedly. 'Aren't you going to introduce us to your girlfriend?'

'Ladies, this is Camilla Reed. She works for *Voyages* magazine.'

Beth held out her hand, suddenly self-conscious that she hadn't had time to file her nails, let alone put on any polish. Going bowling the night before hadn't helped either.

'This is Beth Allen, consultant in charge of our European development program and Freya Scott, her assistant,' said Jack.

Camilla hesitated a moment before giving Beth's hand a limp shake.

For a moment, Beth wondered if she'd seen Camilla in one of Louisa's magazines. She was so skinny and so beautifully-groomed, maybe she was a model. She was even thinner than Louisa, even though she had to be ten years older. 'Pleased to meet you,' she said, sounding rather bored.

Beth was determined to be polite and friendly. 'So you work for *Voyages* do you? That must be very exciting.'

'It is,' drawled Camilla.

'You could do a feature on some of our tours,' piped up Freya. 'We've just added a dog sledding break to the portfolio.'

Camilla raised a perfectly plucked eyebrow and Beth reminded herself to go and get hers waxed at the next opportunity.

'Dog sledding? How bizarre,' she said, flicking an imaginary speck of dirt from her shimmering mini-dress.

'With real huskies and Sami tents,' added Freya, getting into her stride. 'You get to eat reindeer meat.'

Camilla pulled a face. 'How gross.'

Beth could have sworn Jack had tightened his arm around Camilla's waist. He smiled at Freya. '*Voyages* clients are very up market. Perhaps tents and dog sledding aren't really their kind of thing.'

'Maybe, I could be persuaded to make an exception,' said Camilla suddenly sparking into life. 'In fact, Jack's already issued an open invite to try one of your packages. I'm just waiting to see if I can fit it into my calendar. Have you read *Voyages*?'

'Is that the one that's got a voucher for a free Brazilian?' said Freya.

'Our clients like to be well-groomed, but they usually have their personal waxer take care of um… that kind of thing,' sniffed Camilla. 'I think you're getting us confused. The only Brazilians we feature are luxury spa retreats in the rainforest. Although we did have Gisele try out some eco-friendly cottages in the Grenadines.'

'Who's Gisele?' asked Freya innocently. 'Is she that blonde girl off *Big Brother*?'

'I think the person you're referring to is Chantelle,' said Camilla icily. 'Not our kind of thing at all.'

'What am I like?' giggled Freya. 'But I think she's nice.'

Out of the corner of her eye, Beth could see Marcus making his way over.

'Ohhh,' said Freya. 'Marcus is back. I'm just off to the loo before the band starts. See you in a mo.'

Jack raised an eyebrow. '*The* Marcus?'

'Yes. That's me,' said Marcus, bounding over and holding out his hand.

'I've heard a lot about you from Beth,' said Jack, as they shook hands.

'This is Jack Thornfield, my boss,' said Beth feeling Marcus's arm around her. 'And this is Camilla Reed.'

'Girlfriend?'

'What a quaint term,' sniggered Camilla.

'So, Marcus, are you up here for the weekend?' asked Jack, as Beth silently prayed for the band to start up again.

'Yes. I got here tonight. Eventually, that is. I don't know how you stand it. The bloody traffic's terrible and I had to leave the Porsche outside Beth's place.'

'You've got a Porsche?'

'2007 model year actually,' said Marcus proudly. '911 Targa 4. Beth loves it, don't you?' he said.

'It is a beautiful car.'

'Mind you, I don't know if it will be parked outside when we get home. The area round Beth's flat looks a bit on the dodgy side to me.'

'Really? Where do you live?' asked Camilla.

'Camden Town,' replied Beth.

Camilla pursed her lips in horror. 'Oh dear.'

'That's a nice set of wheels,' said Jack quickly. 'I'm sure you'll be OK, if it's got a top end security system too.'

'It's got the best,' said Marcus. 'But it's the neighbors that bother me.'

Jack gave a nod. 'The city can be quite intimidating if you're not used to it.'

'It's not that bad here really,' said Beth.

Marcus snorted. 'Apart from the pollution, the congestion charge, house prices, muggings…'

'That's the price you pay for living in one of the world's great cities, I suppose,' declared Jack.

'Can't see us getting much sleep anyway,' said Marcus to Jack. 'We'll probably be up half the night checking to see if it's still there. Lucky our bedroom window overlooks the street and I managed to get under a streetlight.'

'Sensible move,' he said smoothly. 'As you say, you never know what might happen while you're tucked up in bed together.'

'Jack, I see that guy from the band is waving at you,' said Camilla, her eyes beginning to glaze over. Beth had to stop herself sighing with relief as Freya got back for the loo.

'That's Tom. We'd better go and congratulate him on his bass playing,' said Jack. 'Bye ladies—and Marcus. Enjoy your evening.'

'We will,' said Freya, with a noisy slurp that drained the last dregs of her cocktail. Beth watched Camilla steer

Jack towards the stage by means of a beautifully manicured hand on his rear.

When they were out of earshot, Marcus grinned at her. 'You know, I think I might have a pint this time and get in a round. That Dave bloke's all right, by the way. He wants to get my opinion on his perf tubes, so if you don't mind me scooting off for a bit. I think I might get in a round first. What're you having?'

'Kamikaze,' said Beth, trying for oblivion.

Freya giggled as the band launched into the Kaiser Chiefs' 'I Predict a Riot.' 'Well, If you're going to force me,' she shouted, standing on tiptoe to reach his ear. 'I'll have a Screaming Orgasm.'

At the end of the gig, Beth and Freya were queuing for the toilets when Camilla joined them at the front of it.

'Oh dear, were people waiting?' said Camilla, as mutterings rumbled from the end of the line.

Freya's eyes widened. 'Well…'

Camilla shrugged. 'I'm sure they'll get over it. Needs must, but I wouldn't even *dream* of using a loo in a place like this unless I was utterly desperate.'

'It's OK. The Bird is one of the nicer pubs round here,' said Beth.

'I wouldn't know. I don't frequent pubs if I can help it.' She glanced up at Beth, her eyes gleaming. 'But Jack was *so* insistent that we ought to put in an appearance at his office social that I hadn't the heart to say no. He is *so* wonderful with his employees. You must feel very lucky to have him as your boss.'

'Privileged,' murmured Beth as they reached the front of the queue.

Camilla's eyes widened as they got inside the loos. 'Oh. My. God. This is totally gross! It's absolutely villainous in here!'

'I know it's a bit basic, but look, why don't you go first and get it over with?' offered Beth, almost feeling a bit sorry for her.

Camilla shuddered but strode in front anyway, kicking open the door with her shoe.

'Oh dear,' whispered Freya, as the cubicle door slammed shut. 'There's no loo seat in that one and I think there's something ever so rude written on the back of door.'

—⁓—

Jack was standing at the bar, having decided to get in a round for the band while Camilla was 'powdering her nose.' He turned to find Marcus behind him, smiling broadly. Close up, he realized the bloke was a good inch taller than him. He was very blonde too, and Jack was bizarrely reminded of a young Paul Bettany.

'Can I get you a drink?' he asked.

'I'll get these,' said Marcus. 'Stella, is it?'

'Yeah. Thanks.'

'Missus deserted you, then?' said Marcus after handing over the money to the barman.

'Little girls room,' said Jack.

Marcus rolled his eyes. 'Mine too.'

'How long have you been with Beth?' said Jack casually, leaning against the bar as if he was a regular.

'Years,' said Marcus. 'We went to the same school.'

He nodded in what he hoped was a nonchalant way. 'So you were childhood sweethearts then?'

'Wouldn't say that exactly. We only started going out after her dad had the accident, but to be honest,' he said, lowering his voice as if Beth might appear at any moment, 'she always had the hots for me at school. In fact, if she hadn't taken it into her head to go off round the world, we'd have got together long ago.'

'Right… so it's pretty serious between you, is it?' said Jack.

'Yup. Hope to make it formal any day. Now I've got the business running really well, got a decent five-bed place and all that, I think it's high time I settled down and made an honest woman of her.' He paused to sip his beer. 'As soon as she gets all this London business out of her system of course—not that any of it was necessary.'

'But I thought she needed the money to send her sister to drama school?'

'Well. I could have helped them out, naturally,' he said, shaking his head. 'But she won't hear of it. Nice girl, Beth, if misguided. Well-intentioned but stubborn. Needs careful handling, but I think I've got the knack with her.'

'I'm sure you have,' said Jack, hardly able to believe his ears. Desperate to fight her corner, but unsure how far he dare go as her boss. Because, he told himself, that's all he was as far as Marcus or anyone else was concerned. 'But, you know, this job means more to her than the money. She's doing a great job of developing our European sector. I need her… the company needs her, that is. She's a very dedicated and talented product manager.'

Marcus gave a little snort. 'Hmm. Well, I'm sure she's been very helpful to you, but this is just a temporary blip,' he said, waving his glass dismissively at the pub and at, Jack suspected, Beth's London life in general. 'I know you're her boss, mate, and you're thinking of how you'll manage without her, but with all due respect, in a month or so, she'll be back where she belongs.'

'And where's that?' said Jack, boiling inside. 'With all due respect?'

Marcus looked incredulous 'At home with me. Where else would she want to be?'

Jack picked up his glass and flashed a brief smile at Marcus. 'I'm sure you're right. Nice meeting you,' he said, spotting Camilla beckoning him frantically from the pub door.

'You too, mate. Give me a call if you ever want a decent set of wheels. I could fix you up with a fantastic deal on a BMW Seven series.'

'Cheers.'

Moments later, Beth joined Marcus and kissed him on the cheek. 'Was that Jack you were talking to?' she asked.

'Yeah. He seems all right I suppose. Got some funny ideas about women, but I suppose you won't have to put up him for much longer.'

She spotted Jack at the pub door, draping his jacket around Camilla's shoulders. She squeezed Marcus's hand and smiled. 'Shall we go home now?'

CHAPTER 14

THE TRAIN SLOWED ON ITS APPROACH TO KENDAL STATION as Beth headed back to the Lakes the following Friday night. Over to the west, she could just make out the jagged outline of mountains against an indigo sky. A very different skyline to the one she could see every day from the windows of her office. Without her even realizing it, she'd managed to become fond of both. Concrete and glass, swathed in a heat haze, were now as familiar to her as fells shrouded in mist.

She knew Marcus wouldn't have approved of such thoughts even if he might not say so out loud. Their weekend in London hadn't been great, to say the least. She'd taken him shopping and on the London Eye. He'd admired the engineering and moaned about the queues, but she could hardly blame him for feeling out of place or expect him to do more than tolerate her city lifestyle.

Now she need only jump on the local train to Windermere, get a bus to the village, and she'd be home, she thought with relief. Not even the thought of Camilla and Jack being so… intimate, could dampen her pleasure at seeing her family.

'Tickets please.'

The train manager was smiling down at her. 'Can I see your ticket, love?' asked the woman as she stamped the ticket of another passenger.

Fumbling in her backpack, she found the ticket and held it out. 'Sorry—I was on another planet.'

'Hard week?' said the manager.

'Complicated.'

'Nearly home now though. We'll be in Kendal in five minutes.'

The woman continued on her way up the carriage which was almost empty now apart from a businessman folding up his laptop and a girl with dreadlocks, already standing by the door with her mountain bike.

Beth turned back to the window. It had been a pretty heavy week, quite apart from entertaining Marcus. She'd spent a lot of time researching the Corsican trip and had even run a quick web survey of existing customers to find out the type of activities they might enjoy. Freya had been on a course for most of the week, and Beth was wondering if she could cope with such a major project on top of her own workload. What if she let the company down? She set her jaw. No, she *had* to make the project work. She was determined to prove she could handle it. To herself and to Jack.

The train manager's voice crackled into the carriage, telling passengers they were now at Kendal, urging them not to leave their belongings behind, wishing them a safe onward journey. She felt like adding to the list of instructions as she got to her feet: 'As for that girl in the middle carriage, cheer up and get a life. There are others worse off than you. And stop thinking about your boss.'

After hauling her bag out of the luggage rack, she stood by the doors, trying not to lurch against the businessman. The doors hissed open and she was there. Another train platform, another wait. Half an hour to kill before her train to Windermere arrived.

Staring out over the deserted platform, she felt the cool night air against her face. No heat rising from pavements here; the temperature was several degrees lower than in London.

The street lights were on and the station kiosk had long since closed when Beth finally arrived. She was really tempted to call a taxi but couldn't justify the expense, so she trekked out to the bus stop, hoping she wouldn't have long to hang about. She was trying to decipher the timetable, which was tricky when it was obscured by a message that read, 'Baz shags bus drivers.'

'Beth!'

In the bus stop, Honor, wearing a skirt that brushed the top of her thong sandals, was standing by Daisy.

'Over here!' she called.

'Hi, Honor! What brings you here at this time of night? A secret mission for hot dog rolls?'

Honor laughed from deep down in her chest, sending her dangly earrings wobbling. 'No, a mercy mission to collect a weary homecomer.'

'Did my dad ask you to come by any chance?'

Kissing Beth on the cheek and grabbing her bag, Honor's smile crinkled the corners of her eyes. 'No. I volunteered for the assignment. I was having a bite to eat with him and Louisa when you called.'

Beth wondered if Honor had been feeding the whole family while she'd been away. She seemed to have been spending a lot of time at the bike shop lately, according to Louisa. Beth had seen her briefly on her previous visit home and she'd picked up the phone more than once when she'd had called home. Once, she'd even answered her dad's mobile.

'It's out of your way,' she said, smiling.

'Not really.' Honor indicated a pile of boxes on the back seat. 'I had to retrieve some glasses and crockery from a party. Killed two birds with one stone, if you know what I mean. Not that you're a bird or need killing.' She frowned at Beth's half-hearted smile. 'Get in, love.'

She followed Honor and her skirt towards the car, wondering how she rustled up meals for hundreds of walkers and riders and tourists in that much material. The boot was full of paper plates and cups.

'Do you mind slumming it with your bag on your lap?'

'It's absolutely fine. I've traveled in worse things than Daisy.'

'How's London?' said Honor.

'Gill's flat is great. The job involves a lot of traveling, but I must admit, experiencing all those new places is ten times better than having to stay in the office.'

Honor nodded. 'Gill was always good to your mum. And I'm glad to hear it all sounds wonderful—are you sure you'll want to come back at the end of your contract?'

'I'm sure.'

'Are the natives at Big Outdoors that scary?' laughed Honor.

'Not all of them,' said Beth, laughing. 'There's Freya, my assistant who is an absolute scream. You will *have* to meet her. Tom and Shreeya aren't scary either—they're both product managers. Tom's in a band called Bluesky who are pretty good actually and Dave Stirling, the IT manager is a total geek, but a real laugh… and then there's Brad Pott.'

Honor looked completely confused. 'Brad Pott?'

'Our cactus. Best not to ask.'

Honor chuckled as the van pulled away from the curb. They were nearly home before Beth plucked up the courage to ask what had been occupying the other half of her mind on her way north.

'Has Marcus has been round to the shop since he came down to London?' she asked.

'I haven't seen him myself, but I believe he has.'

'Do you know what he wanted?'

'He didn't stay long, apparently, once he knew you weren't there.'

'Oh.'

Honor sounded amused. 'Tell me to mind my own business, but you could do worse than Marcus, you know.'

Beth clutched her bag as they rounded a sharp bend by the lake shore. The stone wall had a gap in it like a child missing its front teeth.

'If he's the man you want, I wouldn't keep him waiting too long, not that it's any of my business,' added Honor as she accelerated out of the bend. '*If* he is the one…'

'I do like Marcus…' she said, feeling awkward but knowing Honor was only asking questions she knew she'd have to answer herself. Marcus hadn't come straight out with the Big Question last weekend, but one day soon, she just knew he would. Her reply died in her throat; she had no answer for Honor or Marcus. Not yet.

'It's OK, I can see I should mind my own business,' said Honor before tactfully moving on to the latest village gossip. They stopped halfway home, to collect the deposit for a function from a community hall. Alone in the car, Beth thought back to the flowers on the table, the sparkling windows, the well-stocked freezer full of meals in foil trays. Honor had become an important part of her family's life while Beth was away. She and her mum had known each other since their schooldays and Beth couldn't remember a time when the two of them hadn't been together. She and Louisa had always looked on her as a surrogate auntie, although Honor would have thrown up her hands in horror at being referred to as auntie.

'OK,' said Honor, jumping back into the driving seat, waving a check. 'Now I shan't have to send the heavy mob round to the Women's Institute.' She revved the engine hard and they set off. A short time later, they'd reached Wheels on Fire and Honor was heading away up the street, an ominous plume of dark smoke trailing from Daisy's exhaust.

Right now, the stone and slated shop-cum-house, built before the bicycle had ever been invented, seemed as inviting as the grandest palace. As she walked up the path, the smell of fish and chips drifted through the open window, then the front door opened and her dad stood there, leaning on a stick *and* smiling. Well, she thought, as she kissed him on the cheek before hugging an excited Louisa, that was a double improvement.

Marcus arrived on Saturday morning as she was standing in the bath, covered in hair removal cream, legs bowed like a Wild West gunslinger. His arrival was heralded first by the squeal of brakes outside the shop, and second by Louisa, calling knowingly up the stairs.

'Be-eth!'

She froze. Bugger. She only had her knickers on. 'I'm up here, Lou!'

'Someone to see you-uuu!' called Louisa.

'I'll be down in a few minutes,' she shouted through the

bathroom door. After scraping off the cream and hastily rinsing her legs, the bathroom smelled like a chemical plant and there was gunk all over the enamel. Her dad would have a fit, but she didn't want to keep Marcus waiting any longer. Dragging on shorts and an old T-shirt, she bounded downstairs two at a time and found him in the little living room, standing in front of the slate hearth with his arms folded.

'Sorry—doing my legs' she said, leaning over to kiss him. 'I wouldn't get too close, not if you don't want to be knocked out by chemical fumes.'

Marcus wrinkled his nose and backed off slightly.

'Do you want a drink? A beer? Coffee?'

'I'm driving and anyway, I can't stay long. I've got to see a man about a Bentley. I just came over to ask what time you'll be at the Grange tonight.'

She felt her heart flip. 'I'm not sure. You see, I really ought to spend some time with Dad and Louisa.'

He frowned. 'I had hoped we'd spend the night together.'

'Well, I could come over for dinner and then I could come home. Or maybe we could go to the pub here in the village,' she suggested.

Marcus turned his car keys over in his fingers. 'It wasn't what I had in mind, but I suppose it'll have to do. I'll collect you at eight.'

Beth smiled, but inside she felt a growing sense of unease. She *could* have gone over to the Grange; her father wouldn't have minded really and Louisa was out with some friends from the Boat Club. So why hadn't she said yes?

Maybe she needed space, physical space to get things straight in her mind. To think and make sense of the changes in her life over the past few months.

Marcus jangled his keys impatiently.

'I'll see you later then,' she murmured, suddenly feeling weighed down by guilt and uncertainty.

He just shrugged. 'Eight then.'

As she showed him out into the street, he hung about in the doorframe. 'By the way,' he said, pointing at her legs with his car key, 'Haven't you missed something?'

He was clicking the key to the Porsche as she glanced down and saw a stripe of pink cream from her knee to her ankle.

CHAPTER 15

'DO YOU REALLY NEED ALL THIS WEIRD STUFF?' ASKED Louisa as Beth got her kit together later that day for the Corsica trip the following weekend. She was desperate to do something, anything, to take her mind off the previous evening she'd spent with Marcus.

Beth nearly fell off the stool as Louisa offered to help. Lounging on a floor cushion, examining her nails, her sister looked like a Roman noblewoman waiting to be fed a grape. She stepped over a pair of long legs to reach a bag from the cupboard.

'So are you actually *taking* all this crap?'

'You know I am, Lou. And it's not weird, it's essential kit—as you'd know if you'd ever got out and explored the place you live in.'

'I can't wait to get away!'

Beth smiled. 'That much is clear.'

'I do appreciate what you're doing, you know. Even though I don't say it very often, I'm not such an ungrateful cow.'

Beth froze halfway to her mosquito net. Was this Louisa actually thanking her? A hand on her ankle made her turn round. Those big blue eyes looked back at her and she relented, as she always did.

'I do know how hard you and dad work for me. I know you don't really want to be in London or living in scummy old tents and stuff,' she said.

'Lou, I'm touched by your concern, but don't worry. I don't mind being in a tent and London isn't that bad, actually.'

'"Not that bad"? God, it must be better than this place. Nothing *ever* happens. I can't wait to get out of here.'

'Not long to wait now,' said Beth.

'And the bright lights of Liverpool will beckon. Doncha just love the city?'

'Sometimes…' said Beth thinking of her friends and the good times they'd had, of her trips abroad, what she'd achieved for the company. Inevitably, the image of him, arm around Camilla flew into her mind—and of Marcus's angry face the night before. They'd been sitting in the car outside her house when he'd asked her to move in with him when she finally got back from London. She'd asked for more time to think about their relationship.

'Time? Haven't you had enough of that already?' he'd said coldly.

'I need a bit more,' she'd told him before kissing him on the cheek and opening the door of the car. As she'd walked up the path, the realization had hit her like a sledgehammer that this was the first time they hadn't made arrangements to see each other again. Later, inexplicably, she'd found the tears streaming down her cheeks as she'd got into bed and turned out the light.

She pulled down a pair of flip-flops from the cupboard and managed a smile for at Louisa. 'Sometimes I love London, and sometimes I'd do anything to get out of the place,' she said.

'Why? Is the boss a real prick?'

'Lou!' exclaimed Beth. She swore herself, so couldn't really complain. It was the thought of Jack and that part of his anatomy together that had shocked her.

'More like a prat,' she said.

'A real minger then?'

Grabbing the net, she pulled it down from the cupboard, thinking of Jack. At nearly thirty-five, and with the odd grey hair, Louisa would have thought he was ready for his pension.

'Come on then, what's he like?'

'He's well over fifty with a face like a bulldog swallowing a wasp and that's on a good day.'

Louisa nodded sagely. 'Thought so. All these executive types are mingers. Give me an actor or musician any day.'

'I thought you were going to work at this performing arts school, not pull a fellow student.'

'I *am* going to work,' said Louisa propping herself up on her arms. 'But if I meet someone fit and rich as well, I won't complain.' She eyed Beth thoughtfully. 'You won't forget your moisturizer and a bit of lippy, will you? You never know who *you* might meet on one of your trips. You don't want to come across some gorgeous bloke when you're looking…'

'A total mess?'

'Well, yeah.'

'I'll probably be looking really gross most of the time. It's a working trip not a weekend on the Orient Express. And stop pulling a face. You'll stick like it if the wind changes.'

Louisa put out her tongue. 'You always say that and it never does. By the way, since when did you turn into Mum?'

'The day you were born, Lou-lou.'

Louisa sighed dramatically then got to her feet. As she stood up Beth couldn't help admiring her. She was just like their mum: tall, slender, and pretty in an ethereal kind of way that didn't quite go with living above a bike shop. Beth on the other hand, felt she reflected the location. Once, when she'd been a teenager and carrying a bit of puppy fat, Auntie Gill had helpfully said she was 'built for comfort.' She'd cried into her pillow for ages that night.

'What are you taking to wear for clubbing?' said Louisa suddenly.

She shook her head. 'There aren't any clubs,' she replied firmly. Which wasn't true. There were a few in Porto Vecchio and some open air discos under the trees at one of the beach. She blushed, remembering slipping away with Jack into the dark forest one night, bass pounding in the distance, the faint rustle of other couples up to the same thing. Her stomach—and Jack's bottom—had been covered in mosquito bites afterwards and they'd had a great time rubbing in the antihistamine cream.

'No clubs?' asked Louisa. 'What about parties?'

'There won't be any of those either. I've got a night in a hotel, a business meeting with some local suppliers, then it's off to the mountains.'

Louisa pulled a face and pointed at Beth's well-used walking shorts. 'There's now way you can go to a meeting or a posh hotel in those scuzzy things. What if Hugh Jackman walks in or Orlando Bloom?'

'Or Elvis?'

Louisa sighed dramatically and got up from the floor. 'There is no hope for you. I'm going to march you into the village for some new shorts. There's a brilliant sale on at Rush. They've got some really funky shorts... you should show off your assets, lots of girls would kill for a toned bum like you have.'

Her eyes lingered on her reflection in surprise, seeing herself through new eyes for a moment. Even a few months of excess hadn't totally wrecked what her outdoor lifestyle had achieved naturally, without the torture of the gym or diets. Recently, her face and limbs had acquired a golden tan that she had to admit, made her look healthy.

'I so-oo hate you, you don't even need any St. Tropez,' said Louisa, wistfully. 'And you've got lovely hair that always does what you want. It looks much nicer like that. Are those highlights?'

'Freya said I should let it grow longer and I got the high-lights done by her brother. He's a student at one of the hair and beauty colleges in London. Do you really like them?'

'I do. I can see this Freya knows what she's talking about. We'll have to get together with her and sort you out.'

'You'd like her,' said Beth, grimacing as she noticed the frayed hem on her shorts. They *were* a bit sad.

'Anyway, I can't stop here, helping you all night,' said Louisa, suddenly, tossing her hair. 'I have to go. I've got a date myself.'

'And who might that be with?'

He sister tapped the side of her upturned nose. 'That would be telling.'

'Not that guy from the boat yard?' she asked, picturing Greg turning up at the door. He was almost as old as Beth, had been banned from driving twice, and was often stoned to boot. He also had floppy black hair, chocolate-brown eyes, and a six-pack honed from a life spent restoring yachts. Half the village girls had a crush on him and she didn't really blame them—just as long as he left her sister alone.

'It's not Fit Greg, chance would be a fine thing,' sighed Louisa.

She was halfway through the door before she leaned her head around the frame. 'Be-eth…'

'Yup.'

'At least get your eyebrows waxed before you go off on this trip, just in case your bulldog of a boss does want to shag you…'

Beth was quick but not quick enough. Her flip-flops clattered harmlessly against the door, as Louisa thudded down the back stairs, shrieking.

The next morning, she woke up to the smell of frying bacon. Poking an arm out of the duvet, she fumbled for her watch and she saw the big hand had barely made it past seven. Could Louisa be making breakfast, she wondered. Could she actually have surfaced this early?

Pulling on combats and a T-shirt, she padded barefoot down the narrow back stairs and into the kitchen. The slate floor felt cold under her feet and her nostrils twitched. The aroma grew stronger, accompanied by hissing and spitting. Her dad was standing at the stove, poking a frying pan with a spatula. His metal crutch was leaning across the end of the table. 'Morning, love.'

'Dad—you're cooking.'

'Well spotted, Elizabeth.'

'But—'

'You thought I lived on cold beans out of the tin and charity casseroles from the neighbors?'

'No. Of course not. It's just…'

He reached for the grill pan to rescue some toast, quickly turning his grimace of pain into a smile.

'Let me help you.'

'No. It's all right.'

She took a step forward. 'Dad.'

'Don't fuss, lass.' He shrugged off her arm. 'Sit yourself down.' Then he smiled. 'Or else.'

'Don't call me lass,' she said mechanically. 'Is that a threat by the way?'

'A promise. Leave me be. You know, you don't have to go off and do this job for Louisa. She could get a job, put it off for a year. We might all be back on our feet by then.'

Beth felt strangely hurt.

'Don't look like that. I am grateful for your help. Louisa too—much more than she ever lets on.'

'I'm not looking for thanks. It's what I want to do.'

He sighed. 'Just don't think you have to take on every Allen problem, that's all. We don't want you turning into your mum, do we?'

'We both know that won't happen.' She shook her head, knowing that her dad blamed her mum's worrying for what had happened to her, even though it was total rubbish. Brain hemorrhages weren't caused by worry, they were caused by… the doctors had offered no answers, just professional sympathy.

As she watched her father add some eggs to the pan, she couldn't help thinking back to how she'd felt when her mum had been diagnosed one sunny June day and how rapidly she'd deteriorated—how quickly it had all been over in a matter of hours. She'd been the one who'd stayed calm. She remembered now how she'd held Louisa while Auntie Gill had comforted their dad.

She'd cried, of course she had, but not in public, not even at the funeral. Counseling had been suggested by one well-meaning relative which had made Beth button up her feelings even more. Honor had tried to talk to her, but even then, she hadn't felt able to open herself up and let her true pain out. But why, she'd wondered and still did, did she have to scream to show how she felt? She'd been screaming inside. She shook herself, trying to clear the fog of gloom that was threatening to spoil what was, by recent standards, a Really Good Moment.

Her dad popped a plate of crispy bacon and sausages on the pine table. A thick cottage loaf was already waiting alongside the bread knife. Ridiculously, she suddenly felt tears pricking and had to dig her nails in her palm to stop them. Fortunately he hadn't noticed, he was so busy scooping fat over the eggs to get them perfect. When he turned round with the pan, she searched for something to say, anything to avoid letting her dad see her face. She pointed to a vase of full-bloom yellow roses on the dresser.

'Nice flowers,' she said, as he added the pan of eggs to the table and eased himself into a chair.

'They're all right, I suppose,' he said, dipping a crust in his egg. 'If you like that sort of thing, that is.'

'Did Honor buy them for you?'

'She might have.'

'Well, they're beautiful.'

'Yes,' he said. 'They are. Now don't let your breakfast get cold.'

Beth wolfing down her fry-up far faster than was healthy seemed to amuse her father.

He smiled. 'Do you want some more eggs? I can easily put some on.'

'No thanks. It was lovely, but I just need to pop to the shops,' she said, dropping her plate in the old Belfast sink.

Ten minutes later, she'd managed to nab a pair of Banana Moon shorts from the sale rail in Rush, the village's trendiest outdoor shop. On her way to the till she just couldn't resist adding a little halter top that had fifty percent off. The chances of being able to wear it in the Lakes were slim, but in Corsica, she could practically live in it.

Louisa was right: she owed it to the company to look her best.

CHAPTER 16

ON THE MONDAY AFTER THE GIG, JACK WAS SITTING IN HIS office, trying to make sense of a perfectly ordinary weekend that had left him unsettled. On the Saturday morning, after the gig, he'd kissed Camilla goodbye, seen her safely into a cab then headed off to his brother's place in Windsor. Nick and his wife had shaken their heads when they'd got back from their day out to find him playing Mario Kart with his nephew and niece, amid a sitting room littered with McDonald's Happy Meal cartons.

On the Sunday night, he returned to his apartment to find an answerphone message from Camilla, demanding to know why his mobile had been switched off and would he phone her 'ASAP, Jack, darling.' It had taken lunch at her favorite haunt in Knightsbridge to pacify her.

He wandered over to the window, hoping to find solace among the statement tower blocks poking like accusing fingers into the London skyline. He felt guilty because while he'd been eating sushi with Camilla, a corner of his mind had been reserved for Beth. He just couldn't *believe* she was in love with a bloke like Marcus. Or was that just because he didn't want to accept she liked someone else?

There was no denying it. Over the past few years, he'd become more and more cynical about women—especially since Saskia. He'd grown to believe that all he really needed was a slinky, sexy woman who'd keep him warm at nights. Someone willing to share his weekend espresso, his new Killers album, and his power shower. Because, he thought, that seemed to be as good as it was ever going to get. Now he was staring thirty-five in the face and he wasn't so sure that good coffee, great music, and sex without strings were enough to see him through a lifetime.

Back at his desk, he consoled himself by choosing a victim for a company health and safety course that involved a weekend in Slough. Ten minutes later, he'd narrowed the course down to the marketing manager and the accounts assistant, when Martha came in with his daily fix. Another espresso, another file, and, he noted with quiet pleasure, a Snickers was placed on the edge of his desk.

'Thanks, Martha. I owe you one.'

He pulled a file from his in tray and tried to get down to some real work.

Later in the week, Beth found herself in Jack's office, preparing to run through a presentation and web mailing she'd devised to market the tours to travel agents and the public. Her laptop whirred softly from the table and behind her, a web page was projected onto a white board. The stream of air from the unit above her head set tiny goose bumps rippling across her bare arms. Jack was leaning back in his chair behind his desk, his hands round a mug.

She took a sip from a cup of water, tapped the keyboard pad, and launched into her spiel. 'High street agents aren't going to be first port of call for packages like this as the tours are too specialized,' she explained, focusing on the screen. 'So we'll be focusing by selling it via the web on the business-to-customer side as well as approaching some agents via the web to sell it on business-to-business basis.'

'What's your commission figure for the agents?'

'I've been through the stats thoroughly with Freya and we've decided that we should start off by offering an initial figure of fifteen percent commission. Any less and they won't take any notice. There's some room for maneuver, but not much, or we'll be eating into our margin.'

He nodded approval. 'OK. Shoot with the rest.'

'What you see here is the draft web page,' she said, pointing to the screen which flagged up photos of a family hiking and a group of girls in wetsuits sliding down a cascade into a pool. 'I've also done a draft mailshot to the travel agents, which we can email out.'

Picking up an A4 sheet, she started to read aloud as the laptop scrolled through a slideshow of typical sights and activities.

"*Dear Agent, Big Outdoors is pleased to announce the launch of a new Adventure Product in partnership with Lorenzelli Tours. Called 'Corsica Escape,' this concept offers the perfect mini-package for those travelers looking to start their first travel adventure in a smaller way…*"

She paused as he sat back in his chair. 'Carry on, sounds good so far,' he said.

She stood up taller in the new kitten heeled slingbacks Freya had persuaded her to get. 'Um… to continue. "*One of the great things about traveling with Corsica Escape is that it's very much like traveling independently, but with none of the drawbacks.*"

'A strong USP,' he said. 'An adventure but not quite. Like it.'

"*Passengers are free to do as they choose; to pursue their own interests one day or take part in activities or sightseeing Corsica Escape has arranged the next. Our leaders in Corsica have many years of experience and really know their clients' needs. We can assure your customers of a great adventure and wonderful experience.*" She finished with a flourish, beginning to almost enjoy herself.

He stayed silent for a few seconds as she finished by clicking on a short video clip of a couple hiking over a ridge.

'Well?' she asked when the clip had ended.

'Where are my hiking boots?' he said, breaking into a grin. 'You've convinced me. In fact, you've made me want to get out of this place right now and catch the first plane out. It's a great pitch, both on the customer and agent side,' he said, his grin fading to a wry smile. 'Even at fifteen percent commission.'

'I could push for less, but experience tells me they won't bite.'

'Relax. I trust your judgment. I'll just have to cancel the Bentley, I guess.'

She laughed, felling a small wave of relief flow over her as he gestured to the small table overlooking the window. 'Want some Goji berries?' he asked, pulling out a packet from the drawer. 'They have five hundred times the Vitamin C of oranges… or so I'm told.'

As he offered the bag, her eyes were drawn to his arms. He had his sleeves rolled back up to below his elbows. White shirt, tanned wrist, chunky watch: it was a perfectly ordinary combo, but it made her throat feel dry.

'Thanks,' she said, even though she'd had so many that week, she thought she might barf. Jack shook a few onto her palm.

'Aren't they a bit on the healthy side for you?' she couldn't resist adding after she'd managed to swallow them. Jack threw the empty packet in the bin and sat down at his desk.

He folded his arms. 'Are you implying I'm a couch

potato? That I'm out of shape?' He looked stern, but his eyes, crinkling sexily at the corners, gave the game away.

Desire stirred low in her stomach and she shook her head, trying to relax her tautening muscles. 'No, you look really fit. I mean, you look um… very well. It's just, you like your chocolate and…'

He had his head on one side, his eyebrows raised, as she dug a deeper and deeper hole. Then he laughed. 'You're right. I ought to get out of the office more, but it's just not practical at the moment. In the States, I used to jog a couple of miles before work, but here in London, it's all I can do to get to the gym a few times a week.'

'Where were you based?'

'San Francisco. Our office had a view of Alcatraz.'

'That must have concentrated your mind.'

'To stay on the straight and narrow?' he asked.

'Something like that.'

'How's Marcus?' he asked, startling her.

She recalled their last conversation with a little skip of her heart. 'He's OK. Very busy with the dealership and he's thinking of running for the district council too.'

'That doesn't surprise me.' He paused. 'You must miss your family when you're down here.'

She glanced at him in surprise. 'Of course I do, but dad seemed well on the mend when I went home at the weekend and Louisa is always bubbly. Overconfident, full of herself, dreaming of bad boys…'

'How bad?' asked Jack, getting up and walking to her side of the desk.

'Very,' she murmured, the image of Louisa almost skipping up to bed when she'd come back from the boat-yard party. 'Very bad boys indeed. The kind of guy you wouldn't want your sister to have anything to do with.'

'As bad as this?'

He seemed very close to her now. It was more than his physical presence. She could smell him, imagine she felt the heat of his body pressing against hers. Suddenly, his hand was covering her fingers like a warm glove, pulling her to her feet. He was cupping her face in his hands, his fingers and thumbs tilting her chin up to him. She shut her eyes and opened her mouth, wanting him to be a bad boy and kiss her. Wanting to be a bad girl herself and let him. Wondering if that kiss would still taste as sweet after eight long years…

'*Jack.*'

The sound of Martha's voice from the desktop machine had the impact of a fire bell clanging in an elevator. His stomach plummeted to his boots.

'*Jack. I have Camilla waiting on the line for you.*'

In seconds, Beth was across the other side of the room, gathering up papers, banging down the lid of her laptop with a click. 'Have to get back to work,' she mumbled, dropping a folder on the floor in her haste to get out of the room.

'*Jack! Camilla says it's urgent. Can you pick up? Are you there?*'

He grabbed at the phone, which clattered nosily against the desk before he snatched it up again. 'Yes, Martha. I'm here!'

Beth heard him call after her as she headed for the door. 'Wait, please!'

By the time she'd made it back to her office via the ladies, she'd managed to bring her breathing back to normal. Freya had gone to lunch, leaving her a note on her desk asking if she wanted a sandwich or sushi. Right now, she felt she couldn't eat anything ever again.

Jack had touched her, he'd been about to kiss her…

Wrong. She'd had been about to kiss *him*. In fact she realized, with shock, she might have gone a whole lot further than a kiss if Camilla hadn't called. A Camilla whose feet seemed to be so firmly under Jack's table that she could get put straight through to his office any time she liked.

CHAPTER 17

JACK SPENT A GOOD WHILE BEFORE RETURNING CAMILLA'S call, trying to catch his breath after what had happened with Beth. He asked Martha to field his calls and by two-thirty, the BLT bagel she'd had ordered for him, lay untouched on his desk. He might have known Camilla didn't really need him urgently. She'd only wanted to ask if the *Voyages* photographer could call at short notice to get a shot of him in his office, but Beth wasn't to know that.

'What a bloody mess,' he muttered under his breath.

He knew he should never have touched her and that he should be grateful that Camilla had called him and put a stop to what was totally unprofessional behavior. But he wasn't grateful and that scared him more.

He pulled a file towards him. Inside was a memo attached by a clip to a thick wad of paper. It was a summary of Beth's itinerary for her Corsican visit. Questions she was going to ask, statistics on visitor numbers, profiles on competitor firms, ideas for promoting tours. All, he noted, very thorough, just as he'd expected. On the last page was a post-it note written in her small, rounded handwriting.

Jack,
I've tried to cover everything but if there is anything
else you think I've missed, let me know ASAP.
Beth

He caught his breath as he reread the words, tracing the writing with his fingers, feeling how hard she'd pressed the pen into the post-it note. She must have mixed feelings about going, he knew that, yet she'd produced a great marketing pitch in spite of everything. He frowned slightly at her words. *Anything she'd missed?* His heart began to beat a little harder in his chest. Was he missing something here? Was he expecting too much of her, sending her off to handle a big project like this on her own?

Dropping the uneaten bagel in his desk drawer, he reached out a hand to press the buttons on his phone. Next door, in the admin suite, Martha was enjoying a nice cup of fruit tea and a rare moment of peace. She was reading the latest *Richard & Judy* book club recommendation and finding it rather affecting. Just as she'd got to a particularly crucial moment, her desk phone buzzed. She reached out and flicked the button, her eyes not leaving the page.

Jack's voice, a definite edge to it, cut through her quiet office. 'Martha, would you mind popping in here?'

'Hmm…' Martha flicked the page. She just couldn't wait to find out what happened next.

'That's right now if you can, Martha!'

She jumped. 'Oh—sorry. Yes, er… on my way.'

Muttering under her breath, she wiped a small puddle of raspberry tea off the corner of the jacket and reluctantly put away the book in her desk drawer.

Inside his sanctum, Jack was standing by his window, arms folded, feet square. He saw the door open and Martha entered, looking as blameless as Mother Teresa.

'Good bit was it?' he asked.

'As a matter of fact yes. Would you like to borrow it?'

He laughed. 'Maybe another time. Sorry to disturb you.'

She glanced away. 'How can I help you?' she murmured.

'I'd like you do some rearranging of my calendar over the next two weeks, please.'

She looked puzzled. 'Well, that could be very tricky. You know you have a meeting with Sir Robin Brinton timetabled?'

'I know. Reschedule it. Send my apologies and um… say I have a memorial service to attend.'

'Would that be a family friend?' asked Martha innocently.

'Second cousin,' replied Jack, straight-faced. 'On my mother's side. We were quite close at one time.'

'I'll make a note of it when I email Sir Robin's PA. What about the quarterly finance meeting?'

'Delegate it to Craig Turnbull. It's time he had more responsibility. I can't always be here to hold his hand.'

Martha nodded, a slight smile forming at her lips. 'And the motivational exercise with the French operations team?'

'Send them out to Café Rouge for the afternoon.'

There was a silence. 'That was a joke, I take it?'

He couldn't keep a straight face any longer. 'Yes—but only just. Arrange a breakfast meeting for us all at seven am next Tuesday. That should get their juices flowing.'

'No problem. Shall I reschedule the rest of your meetings?'

'Yes, if you would.'

He found himself hesitating as his PA waited for further orders. He had a momentary wobble about what he'd decided to do. Suddenly, he wasn't sure it was a good idea.

'Jack, I don't mind re-arranging your schedule, but is everything OK?'

'Everything's fine,' he said firmly.

'So can I do anything else for you?'

'Yes, you can, as a matter of fact. Book me on a plane to Corsica. I'm going on the scouting trip with Beth Allen.'

As Martha left the office, he knew she would be wondering why he wanted to go to Corsica when he had an important meeting and a list of jobs as long as his arm to do. However, the more he thought about it, the more he managed to convince himself that he had no choice but to go along. Beth was a very competent manager, but on the other hand, she was relatively inexperienced, still, at supplier liaison. Olivier Lorenzelli would make the whole package seem so tempting. Maybe he'd make it seem too tempting, reasoned Jack. It was a major sector, a vital new addition to the program, there was so much at stake…

Towards evening, Martha knocked on his door again.

'I had a bit of a job getting you on the same flight, but I've managed it. Your flights leave tomorrow morning,' she explained. 'I booked you into economy. I hope that's OK because you did say we should be tightening our belts.'

'It will be fine. I'm grateful for your work, Martha. You're a miracle worker.'

Martha's face was a picture. 'Thanks.'

'I'm going on this trip because it will be good for me to get back into the field and see what we're all about. In fact,' he added, with what he thought was a touch of genius, 'I'm planning to get out with each of the product managers over the course of the year. This will be my only chance while Beth Allen's here. Her contract only has a few more weeks to run.'

'You do as you think best,' said Martha, surprised that he was justifying himself to her. 'And maybe that's a good idea, not that it's any of my business. The last MD, for what's it's worth, hardly set foot outside London and didn't really understand what the staff have to contend with—that was one of the problems.'

She looked embarrassed at voicing her opinion so boldly. 'Here's the itinerary. You're staying at the Mare I Monti tomorrow night—that's a small but characterful hotel which I hope meets with your approval. After that,

I presume, you'll be making your own arrangements with the supplier.'

'Thanks, Martha, for the arrangements and the support. And go home now.'

'But it's only quarter to five.'

'I said go home. Call it working time sovereignty.'

Martha looked puzzled. 'That's corporate-speak for bunking off on boss's orders,' he said.

She smiled. 'Ah… well, thanks. Good night.'

As she left the office he saw the pleasure on her face— and as for her small and cozy hotel, it sounded just perfect.

CHAPTER 18

THE SUN BOUNCED DOWN OFF THE TARMAC AS BETH HANDED over her company credit card to the taxi driver and headed for the Heathrow departure lounge. The day had finally arrived when she was heading to Corsica. There would be memories she'd rather forget, that was true, but there were also going to be big compensations—like getting out of the office, meeting new people, and bringing to fruition a project she'd been working hard on for weeks.

What's more, the air felt warm on her bare arms, her rucksack felt reassuringly solid on her back, and her feet were—just feet, not alien creatures bent at unusual angles and forced into pointy toes.

Inside the departure hall, the check-in queue was already snaking back from the desk. It was an eclectic mix of travelers, she noted with a professional eye. Mostly middle-class families taking the kids away before state school holidays began, silver-haired couples 'spending the kids' inheritance,' and the odd backpacker. She slotted in behind a family whose twin girls, according to their mini-Samsonites, were called Tallulah and Lavender. After checking in her backpack and grabbing a frappuccino from the coffee bar, she headed back outside to phone Louisa. She punched in the number, one hand over her ear to drown out the roar of jets.

'Hi there.'

She didn't have even have to look up to know whose the voice was.

'There's been a slight change of plan,' said Jack. He was wearing shorts, boots, and a black T-shirt. He had a rucksack on his back and a pair of dark glasses pushed back on his head. She gulped. He looked so sexy, so like the Jack she'd loved and lost that she almost forgot the years had passed. A sudden breeze rippled across the forecourt, setting goose bumps pricking her arms and she was reminded of how much time had gone by since she'd first known him.

'This had better not be what I think it is,' she said, heart pounding.

'Just what do you think "this" is?'

'That you didn't have enough confidence in me to let me handle this trip on my own.'

He shook his head. 'I promise I'm not checking up on you. I'm here to help.'

'It looks a bit like you are. Checking up, I mean, not helping. I don't mean that you're not trying to help but...'

she stopped, aware that he was definitely not the old Jack, but her managing director. 'I just mean that I *can* handle this project on my own.'

He just smiled and flipped a thumb towards the terminal building. 'Come on.'

'So it's final. You are coming with me,' she said as they headed for the check-in desks.

'Yes, I am.'

'Buy why, Jack?'

He shrugged off the pack. 'I've thought about whether I should come with you very carefully and I promise you, we'll discuss it—but not right now. Check-in's closing in fifteen minutes.'

Over at the check-in desk one or two stragglers were handing over bags. 'Then you'd better be quick.'

He dropped his pack onto the tiles and dug out his passport and tickets. 'Wait for me in the departure lounge,' he said.

Beth passed through security in a daze and found a seat in the crowded lounge, her mind working overtime on what to make of his appearance. Immediately she dismissed one possible motive. Even after their near kiss in the office, he couldn't possibly want to renew their relationship. She was still, technically, with Marcus, even if things were rocky between them, and in a few weeks, she'd be back home for good. A sudden, insistent beep from her phone made her jump. Once she'd fathomed out the text, she smiled at it.

'Message from Marcus?' asked Jack, arriving at last.

She pressed the clear button. 'Um… no… as a matter of fact, it's from my sister.'

A garbled message crackled out above their heads. 'That's our flight, I think,' he said. 'Looks like I just made it.'

'So it seems.'

He smiled benignly. 'After you.'

In front of them Tallulah and Lavender were proudly bearing tiny shopping bags from Gap. They twisted their heads, staring at Jack. He pulled a funny face and they giggled in tandem. Their mother, a polished redhead in white cropped jeans, turned round and eyed him suspiciously. He winked at her and her lips pursed in disgust. Their mum grabbed her twins' arms, and yanked them, protesting, towards passport control.

'We can have a good chat on the plane,' said Jack as they shuffled down the sky-bridge.

'But we won't be able to sit together. We didn't check in at the same time.'

He smiled. 'Hmm, could be a problem. Have to see what I can do. We definitely need to be together.'

As she found her seat by the window and buckled up, he lingered at the front talking to one of the female crew members. A few moments later, a harassed-looking woman carrying a squirming baby sat down next to them with an apologetic look. Immediately, the baby started yelling fit

172

to burst her eardrums. Jack was still at the front of the plane talking to the crew and a tall thin man in a business suit who was wrinkling up his nose and nodding.

She grinned at the baby which yelled even louder.

'Sorry to move you, but mind if I take the middle seat?' said Jack, appearing in the aisle.

'You might regret it,' said the mother, looking pained.

'No worries,' he said. 'Let me hold her while you get up.'

When he'd handed back the baby, he wriggled his way into the narrow aircraft seat, knees squashed hard against the magazine pocket. The baby howled as the cabin attendant tried to strap it into its harness.

'How did you manage that?' she said against his ear.

'I had a word with the crew manager. She persuaded a guy to swap this for a quieter seat. Looks like he made the right decision.'

'For him, maybe,' she hissed.

'It certainly looks like we'll have to take a rain check on the work until we get to the hotel,' he said as the baby began to roar louder than the engine.

Beth smiled at the mother and tried to imagine she was somewhere else because soon, she realized, she had far more to distract her than a restless baby. Her thighs were pressed very firmly against Jack's and every time either of them moved the hairs on his arms tickled her skin and set off an annoying tingle. As the engines throbbed and the plane tore down the runway, the baby howled louder. Jack

173

pulled the safety card from the seat pocket and wafted it at the shocked baby which stopped crying and started staring at him from huge blue eyes.

'Thanks,' said the mother gratefully. 'She's been grizzling all morning. Bit of a bug coming on possibly.'

'Could be her teeth. She looks about the right age…' said Jack, tickling the baby under the chin.

'Do you always have this effect on women?' said the mother flirtatiously, as her little girl chuckled. Beth rolled her eyes.

'Rarely, if ever,' he said.

—⁓—

The Mediterranean light was blinding as the plane touched down in Figari. It bounced off the dusty runways, off the white planes and the airport building. The heat hit her the moment she shuffled out of the plane and onto the concrete runway, the smell of diesel fighting with the faint tang of herbs drifting off the maquis at the edge of the airfield. In the melee of excited passengers, she found she'd outstripped Jack and by the time she'd got to the single security guard, he was several passengers behind. Once into the departure lounge, she disappeared into the Ladies. One glance in the mirror showed her pink and flushed cheeks and dry lips—and none of the effects had anything to do with the flight. Splashing a paper towel with water, she held it on her cheeks, feeling the cool moisture against her skin.

She kept telling herself that she could handle being here in Corsica with Jack again. She still had no idea how it had happened. All she knew was that history wasn't going to repeat itself. Jack wasn't going to rekindle any passion between them. He wasn't going to make her fall in love with him. And he wasn't going to leave her, inexplicably. Ten minutes later, she did her best to stroll coolly into the arrivals hall to find him standing by an advertising board, talking into his phone. He finished his conversation and thrust the phone back in his pocket.

'Jack! *Bonjour*!'

A shout from the doors made them both turn their heads. A tall, lean man, with a ponytail and blond streaks in his hair was walking over, arms outstretched. He reminded Beth of Johnny Depp in *Pirates of the Caribbean*.

'Olivier! How are you, mate?'

'*Tres bien*, indeed… mate,' said Olivier. Beth noticed he had a tiny diamond earstud. He really is Captain Sparrow, she thought, knowing Louisa would have been in a pool of drool. He hugged Jack enthusiastically and landed kisses on both cheeks that almost echoed around the arrivals hall. No one took a bit of notice. She stood by politely, smiling inwardly at he tried to look cool about being hugged and kissed.

'And who's this you have brought with you?' asked Olivier, releasing Jack with a final whack on the back and holding out his arms to her.

'This is Beth Allen, our new consultant. Meet Olivier Lorenzelli, friend and potential colleague,' said Jack.

'Only potential?' asked Olivier, raising his eyebrows. Jack shook his head as Beth got a slightly gentler bear hug and four kisses. Olivier's tiny goatee tickled her cheek and he smelt faintly of peppermints. 'So. You are staying at the Mare I Monte?'

'Yes. One of your staff recommended it to us. She said it had lots of character and it has a fabulous position up in the old town,' said Beth.

'*Caractère?*' Olivier laughed. 'Yes, it has plenty of that. It is on the edge of the cliff—at the moment. I hope you have a head for heights.'

'I do. Can't wait,' she said as Olivier ushered them out of the airport doors into the afternoon heat.

'Come. I also have someone for you to meet.'

Standing outside, talking on a mobile, was a woman dressed in shorts, a T-shirt, and flip flops. She waved when she caught sight of them. 'This is Marisa Corbières, our operations manager,' he explained.

If Olivier was the skipper of Lorenzelli Tours, Marisa was his trusty first mate. About twenty-five, she was short and olive-skinned with curly black hair. She looked very fit and Beth felt a pang of envy for her obvious outdoor lifestyle.

'I have just been telling Jack and Beth that without you, Marisa, our company is lost,' said Olivier, as Marisa put her phone away.

She shook her head and smiled. 'I wouldn't have described it like that. We have a very good team here. Olivier flatters me.'

'Marisa is accompanying us on the trek,' he replied, as they crossed the airport road towards the car park.

'Thanks for taking the time out. You must be very busy while you're still in peak season,' said Beth to Marisa, as the guys strode on ahead, deep in conversation.

'I don't need an excuse to be out of the office and up in the mountains. I'm looking forward to it.' said Marisa. 'More importantly, we are very happy that Big Outdoors is interested in offering our tours. When you see what we have to offer, I'm sure you'll be pleased.'

Beth's eyes took in the rose-colored mountains rising up in the distance. Whether Jack was here or not, she was going to enjoy herself. 'I already know I'll love it here,' she murmured.

'Ah, have you been to Corsica before?' asked Marisa as Olivier opened the doors of a black SUV with tinted windows.

Beth's cheeks flush as they climbed in the back seat. 'Once—but it was a very long time ago.'

If Jack read anything into her remark, he didn't show it and in a moment, the doors were shut and they were on their way down the dusty access road towards the shimmering coast.

CHAPTER 19

BETH LAY IN HER UNDERWEAR ON HER HOTEL BED, STARING at the ceiling. An ancient fan stirred the air just enough for comfort. She turned her head towards the window, its shutters fastened back against the wall to stop them from clattering in the breeze blowing off the sea.

Pushing herself off the bed, she crossed to the window and peered over the tiny balcony. A hundred feet down the sea broke against the cliffs. She inhaled deeply, the fresh scent of ozone mixing with cooking smells from restaurants. Heights exhilarated her and not even the prospect of sharing the evening with Jack could dampen her spirits. She shaded her eyes, trying to make out the Sardinian coast. Then, sitting back against the bed head, she sipped a bottle of water and tried to read through her notes and itinerary again. She didn't get far because her mind kept focusing on her conversation with Jack after they'd checked in. He'd finally said his piece about why he was here, as they as they'd sat sipping ice-cold diabolos on the hotel terrace while the staff got their rooms ready.

'It's not that I don't think you're capable of handling the trip on your own,' he'd said. 'Or that I don't trust you.'

'But I could have managed,' she'd insisted. 'I've a list of criteria and questions as long as your arm to ask. I won't be swayed by anyone. If the package isn't right in every detail, I'll make sure it's put right before I finally sign it off.'

'Beth—'

'Jack. I've been extremely thorough.'

'I know you have,' he said, taking off his sunglasses so she could see his eyes. 'There are two reasons why I'm here and one of them isn't to do with this trip, not absolutely anyway.'

'I'd love to hear them,' said Beth.

'Think of it like this. I run a travel company and I haven't actually *been* traveling since I started working here. I'm not getting close enough to our core product, and I believe in leading by example. If it's any consolation, I've decided to accompany Tom and Shreeya on two of their supplier recces before the end of the year.'

She wrinkled her nose, unsure whether to believe him or not. 'But what was I to think when you landed at the airport? You could have told me,' she said, swirling the ice nervously in her diabolo, making it chink against the side of the glass. 'I would have guessed you had a million and one things to do that are more important than coming here. I mean you must have had to rearrange your entire calendar and the travel plans. Or has Martha done that?'

'Maybe I should have told you, but frankly, I was by no means sure that I could reschedule my calendar at short notice. But I had an important meeting canceled so I was able to come with you,' he said briskly, indicating there were to be no arguments.

She tried to ignore the feeling they were circling around each other.

'As for your capabilities. Beth, this is a big contract. I don't think it's fair to send you alone and heap the responsibility on your shoulders.'

'So it's not me, it's you...' she murmured, staring at his hands around the glass.

'Don't forget that Olivier and I go way back. It would be silly not to take advantage of the fact that I already have some kind of relationship with him. I *know* him.'

'And I might not?'

The hotel porter appeared by their table. 'Your rooms are ready, monsieur.'

'*Merci*,' he said, draining his diabolo and picking up his bag. 'I'm really not checking up on you,' he said as they'd stepped out of the afternoon heat and into the cool shade of the foyer. 'Try to think of me as more of an observer.'

His warm smile left her teetering on the edge of giving him the benefit of the doubt. His explanation was perfectly reasonable, although the turning up at the airport was hardly textbook. She had a distinct suspicion that he'd been too scared to tell her in advance, but she didn't dare confront him any further. He was the chief exec, after all.

'I'm only here to offer advice and support when you need it. Other than that, think of me as just another guest,' he said as they followed the porter into the hotel.

'That's probably asking a bit much.'

They stopped outside her room.

'I know, but can you try?'

She nodded then pushed the key in the old lock but didn't open the door. It was stiflingly warm on the landing. He reached across her wrist and turned the key for her, nudging the door, brushing against her hand.

'We'll see, but remember who's in charge,' she murmured, stepping inside.

He laughed. 'See you at seven.'

Then he'd carried on to the next landing, his boots thudding nosily on the wooden stairs.

She'd glanced at her hand, still feeling the touch of his fingers now as she lay on her bed, the pen and notes abandoned. Around her, the light had softened and the shadows had lengthened and a glance at her watch had her springing from the bed. She had to get ready for dinner.

She took a cool shower in the antiquated bathroom and wrapped herself in a rough white towel, letting the sea breeze dry her hair. Then she began to unpack her rucksack. Clean underwear, bug repellent, shorts, flip-flops, maps—all of it was pulled out and laid on the bed and floor. Olivier had said she could leave any unnecessary stuff at his office, making sure they could travel as light as possible on the trek. She'd got to the bottom of the pack when she found something she was sure she hadn't put there: an unfamiliar package wrapped in pink tissue paper.

'Now what is this?' she muttered to herself, pulling out the soft tissue and unwrapping the package. Inside was a piece of fabric and she shook it. A post-it note fluttered out of the heart of the material onto the polished wooden floor. As she picked it up, a smile spread over her face.

> *Sis,*
> *Can't have u looking minging 4 Orlando Bloom.*
> *Luv,*
> *Lou-lou xxx*
> *PS Put it on—and text me a pic.*

Carefully, she untwisted the dress and held it up in front of her. It was one of those dresses that were made to be worn crumpled. Soft blue crinkly cotton with a halter neck and a low back. She wondered if she'd seen it on the back of the chair in Louisa's room. She shook her head but still felt touched. Louisa could be a real sweetheart sometimes. Just when you thought she hadn't listened to a word you'd said or didn't care, she did something impulsive like this.

Letting the towel drop to the boards, she shimmied

into the dress. The cotton fabric felt cool and soft on her bare skin even though it clung to all her curves. She pulled open the old door of the old armoire in her room and as expected, found a full-length mirror with an interesting crack across it that split her reflection in two like an old fairground attraction. She had to admit that the blue looked lovely against her tanned skin and her hair looked shiny and glossy, thanks to Freya's magic highlights. Snapping a very weird picture of herself from neck to knees, she sent Louisa a text.

Thx Lou.
Dress is fab. Must go.
Orlando w8ing in bar.
B x

As she watched the message fly off, a knock at the door startled her. A scan of her watch told her it was later than she'd thought.

'Beth.'

She snatched in a breath. It was Jack. She panicked. Did she have time to pull off the dress and get back into her shorts and a clean T-shirt? Even if she did, she didn't know where they were, among the debris scattered over the floor and bed.

'Beth!' he called.

She blew out her breath. Damn it, where were her

shorts? Where were her knickers, for goodness sake! She absolutely couldn't let him in like this. For some reason, the thought of him coming into the room when she was naked under the thin dress made her feel... *vulnerable*. A sudden twist low down in her abdomen made her realize the feeling wasn't unpleasant. The prospect of being caught knickerless by Jack was also unbearably sexy.

He knocked again, louder and more insistently.

'Beth—are you all right in there?' His voice sounded concerned.

All right! What did he think had happened to her in her room? Been kidnapped by Corsican terrorists? Slipped on the soap?

'Hold on a minute!' she cried, still at a loss as to the location of her undies.

The door handle rattled softly.

'I'm here,' she said, pasting on a smile as she tugged open the door.

His expression when he saw the dress said it all. He recovered quickly but she still caught the look. It was definitely surprise, possibly pleasure too; she wasn't quite sure. She was too busy trying to look casual because Jack, freshly showered, shaved, smelling of minty toothpaste, in shorts and a white shirt was as much as she could stand.

'I—I didn't know you were still getting ready...' he hesitated, seeming embarrassed. 'I waited in reception for a while and then I thought you might have lost track of the time or fallen asleep or something. When you didn't answer, I was worried and thought—'

She laughed gently at him. 'I'd fallen off the balcony?'

'Ha ha, very funny.'

'Actually, I've been working and got carried away. Then I had to um... brush my teeth.'

'Oh. Fine. Right. Um... So are you ready to go out then?'

'Yes. I'll just get some shoes and my um... sunglasses,' she said spotting her flip-flops and a pair of knickers poking out from under the pillow.

Turning her back, she cursed as he hovered in the doorway. She slipped on the flip-flops and managed to scrunch up the panties in her fist and push them into a tiny bag.

'Ready,' she said, spinning round to face him.

She saw him watching her. He looked almost mesmerized. 'I can see that.'

He pointed to the bedside table. 'But you've still forgotten your sunglasses.'

She tapped her temple. 'Doh... silly me.'

Jack crossed to the bed, picked them up, then held them out to her. 'Shall we go now?'

A few minutes later, they were threading their way through the narrow streets of Bonifacio towards the steps that led down to the marina. The evening sun still had plenty of heat in it and warmed her bare shoulders. Her hair tickled her skin—she hadn't even had chance to tie it back, as normal, before answering the door. At the bottom of the hill, lining the quayside, cheek-by-jowl with yachts and fishing boats and gin palaces were dozens of restaurants.

'Take your pick,' he said as they lingered on the quayside.

'Oh—anything will do,' she said airily. Anywhere, she thought, with a loo where she could put some underwear on. She pointed to a run-down pizza place next to a tabac. 'What about that one?'

'Are you sure? I think we could find somewhere nicer. After all, we'll have plenty of chances to rough it in the next few days.'

'Of course.'

They ambled along at an agonizingly slow pace, checking out menus and watching waiters buzzing to and fro from kitchens to quaysides, plates piled high with seafood and steaks and pizzas. At last, he pointed to some tables under a canopy up ahead. 'That looks good to me. OK by you?'

'Yes,' she said, trying to hold down her dress discreetly with one hand.

'Are you sure you're not too cold? The wind's got up.'

'Just hungry. Ready for something hot inside me.'

He raised his eyebrows as she gave herself a mental kick. 'Then we'd better get you filled up and fast,' he said, grinning.

She felt his hand on her elbow, motioning her forward. He didn't seem to notice he'd done it, so unself-conscious was the gesture. She shivered in the breeze as the aromas of herbs and garlic mingled with diesel from cars trying to negotiate the narrow marina road.

The restaurant he'd chosen was perhaps the smallest place on the quay and still relatively quiet. The bar and kitchens were housed in what was barely more than a cave—a hollow carved out of the rock cliff face that literally held up the rest of the town above. Moments later a waiter was pulling back a chair for her, handing them two menus, and asking if they wanted an aperitif.

'A beer,' said Jack.

'Orangina.'

He glanced up in surprise.

'I'm thirsty and um—I need the Ladies,' she explained.

'Fine,' he said smiling, though he looked puzzled at how the two were connected.

A few minutes later, she was back. She wriggled a bit on the chair, feeling much safer. 'I'm starving,' she declared, picking up the menu.

Jack shot her a glance that made her tingle from head to toe, then smacked his lips. 'Me too. Absolutely ravenous.'

CHAPTER 20

JACK WAS HAVING IMMENSE TROUBLE CONCENTRATING ON the menu. He'd nearly lost it when Beth had opened the door to her room and he'd seen her in the clingy, floaty dress that showed off her bare shoulders. He also loved the way she'd let her hair fall loose, the way it was tinged golden by the sun.

'*Vous avez choisi?*' asked the waiter.

'*Est-ce que je peux avoir le loup grillé, s'il vous-plaît?*' she replied.

A tiny shiver ran up Jack's spine as he pictured her slipping out of her dress and whispering, in a throaty voice '*Voulez-vous coucher avec moi, Jacques?*' Then he cleared his throat, annoyed with himself for having such cheesy fantasies.

'Monsieur?' said the waiter. ''Ave you decided yet? Do you want ze same as mademoiselle?'

'Grilled wolf?' he stammered, finally working out what she'd ordered.

She giggled. 'Fish. A loup is a type of fish as well as a wolf.'

'Oh. Right. Of course,' he said, squirming inwardly. 'Um… that please,' he said poking a finger at the menu. 'The *plat du jour*…'

'*Rognons blancs?*'

'Yes, please.'

'Is monsieur *certain*?' the waiter asked, looking at Beth with a knowing smile. 'That he wants the—how you say *en Angleterre*—the pig's—er… testeecles?'

She giggled as Jack's face crumbled.

'Jeez, no. I meant that—that one below.'

'Pizza Marguerite?'

'Yes—that'll do. *Merci*.'

The waiter sniffed. 'One pizza for monsieur and *le loup grillé* for mademoiselle.'

'Any wine?'

'A liter of rosé,' said Jack. '*S'il vous plait*.'

'*Bien*.'

The waiter snatched up the menus and returned to the bar, but not before rolling his eyes significantly at Beth. 'Good choice about the wine,' she said when the man had gone. 'Rose goes better with pizza than testee-cles or grilled wolf. You'd want a nice robust red for those.'

He laughed out loud. He didn't care about being teased; he just loved seeing her smile. It relaxed her face and added a sexy sparkle to her grey eyes. Her cheeks were glowing from the sun and she was biting her lower lip, a gesture he found innocent yet strangely erotic. He held out his glass.

'This beer is just great. I'd forgotten how good it was. Here have a taste.'

Condensation trickled down the glass and onto his hand as he offered the beer. She curved her fingers round the slippery glass.

'Try it. It's fantastic,' he urged.

She sipped, flicking a pink tongue over her lips to catch a stray fleck of foam. 'It's good. Very good,' she said, smiling and nodding. 'So sweet and yet so bitter. Do you remember the last time we drank—'

She stopped abruptly, but it was too late because Jack *did* remember. It was one day in their trek. They'd slipped away from the main party to get food and ended up having sex in the heat and dust of shepherd's refuge. Afterwards, almost dizzy with thirst, they'd stopped for a local beer at the bar. Chestnut beer, just like this, with bubbles bursting rich and sweet on your tongue.

'Here's your pizza,' she said quietly.

'I know.'

Having brought the meals, the waiter took a book of matches from his pocket, struck one, and lit the candle on their table.

'*Tres romantique, n'est ce-pas?*' he said, smiling.

191

Beth looked down at her hands so Jack couldn't see her face.

'Could we have some more bread please?' he said politely.

—⁓—

Later, as they wandered back up the steps to the citadel, Beth felt as if her whole body was glowing and she wasn't sure if it was the wine or the steep climb. Their dinner had been so easy and casual and, apart from the waiter assuming they were a couple, it had been the most relaxed few hours she'd spent with Jack since they'd first met. Away from the office, she—and he—seemed to feel free to be themselves. She tried not to think how alike their true selves actually were.

'Marisa seems nice. How long have you known her and Olivier?' she said, making conversation as they neared the city ramparts at the top of the slope.

'Oh, ages. We worked together for a season at a trekking company in the Alps then he moved back here awhile ago.'

'He's very charismatic and charming,' she said, sighing dramatically.

'Charismatic? I shall have to tell him that one. He's a cool customer, is Olivier, and a very clever one. He did an MA in English and History at the Sorbonne.'

'The clients must love him, he's so funny and witty. Kind of ironic—in a sexy French way,' she added wistfully.

He pushed out his lower lip and feigned offence. 'Now, I think you take ze pees out of me, *non*?'

'*Peut-être*. Perhaps *un petit peu...*' she said, trying not to laugh.

'You are vairy naughty, Elizabeth,' he said, wagging his finger at her as she covered her mouth with her hand.

She felt high on wine and laughter as he mimicked Olivier. 'I don't think I can let you take ze pees out of me, Elizabeth. *Peut-être*, think I will 'ave to teach you a leetle lesson, ze French way...'

'Don't you dare!' she cried as he took a step towards her.

He frowned, but his eyes were still laughing. 'Don't dare do what?'

'Carry on talking in that French accent,' she said, not wanting to say what she thought he was going to do.

His face fell. 'And I zought it was zo charming...'

He shook his head and let out a deep laugh that had her heart pitter-pattering, mostly with pleasure, but also because she was afraid she was sliding back the bolts on a place deep inside her heart.

As they reached the ramparts, the sky was almost indigo and over the straits, lights shimmered on the Sardinian coast. The moon made a path on the surface of the water; a broad shimmering lane that she fancied she could almost walk across. Jack leaned back against the sea wall.

'Thought you'd need a rest after that,' he teased.

'What? *Moi*? It looks like *you* need the rest.'

'Hey, I run every day. It's my caffeine habit that makes me so twitchy.'

'And the wine habit? The chocolate addiction? Rumor has it that Martha has a loyalty card at Starbucks and the Sainsbury's Metro.'

He threw her an indignant look. 'Are you suggesting I don't look after myself? My body is a temple, Beth, or will be when we get back. I intend to live a blameless life. Nothing will pass my lips except Goji berries and mineral water.'

She had to put her hand over her mouth to stifle a giggle, as he stood up straight and stiff backed, a solemn expression on his face. It didn't really go with the stubble, jeans, and shirt. Two old men stared at them so he wished them a cheery *'bonsoir'* and pointed in the direction of the narrow streets snaking into the citadel.

'Come on, let's go for a coffee and a nightcap. I know just the place.'

They slipped into the labyrinth of narrow streets. Buildings, five and six stories high, loomed on either side of them, lined with restaurant tables, filled with diners laughing and eating, smoking and talking. Dodging past waiters bearing trays of drinks and food, they climbed steadily until they rounded a corner and she saw the sea again.

There, literally at the top of the town, overlooking a huge black sky sprinkled with stars, was a little cave of a bar. Nightlights flickered on the tables. It was like a tiny, magical grotto and from the way Jack was looking at her right now, they might have been a million miles from home, let alone a thousand.

She ordered *digestifs*—two coffees and two glasses of myrte, the local herb liqueur and for a while, they sat in silence, gazing over the sea to the opposite coast as they waited for their drinks. A tiny spark of hope, as faint and distant as one of the stars, had begun to glimmer in her heart and mind. Did she dare to hope that she'd been wrong about Jack? That he might have changed into a man who was regretful about leaving her, maybe even hoping to renew their relationship?

'It's so beautiful,' she said as the patron placed their drinks on the table.

'Indeed, it is,' he said. 'Idyllic, in fact.'

'Makes you not want to go home.'

'It does makes it difficult,' he said, emptying the contents of a sugar packet into his café crème. 'So, how are things with you and Marcus?'

'How are things with you and Camilla?'

Jack stopped stirring his coffee and laid his spoon carefully in the saucer. 'I guess I asked for that.'

She sighed. 'Marcus and I are… we're trying to make things work, but it's hard with us both being so far apart.'

'I guess it is. Long-distance relationships are incredibly tough. I'm sorry if it's not working out as well as you hoped. Maybe,' he added, 'you can sort it out when you get back home for good.'

'Maybe,' she said, feeling a catch in her throat at being reminded she would soon be out of Jack's world permanently.

'Are things still serious between you and Camilla?' she asked, adding sugar she didn't want to her own coffee so she didn't have to meet his eyes.

He paused so long that she had to look back at him.

'Serious? I'm not sure what that really means,' he said carefully. His eyes seemed to match the midnight sky as the candlelight flickered behind them. 'Do you want to talk about the trip tomorrow?' he asked as a cool breeze gusted in from the sea, rippling the fairy lights.

'I suppose we should really,' she said, her heart sinking. 'We are supposed to be here on business.'

They managed to discuss work for a full ten minutes before the conversation led to Jack's reminiscences of Olivier, then Beth shared some stories about Louisa and her father.

'I think the owner is hinting,' she said as the lights went out, throwing Jack's face into dark shadow. He got out his wallet, fumbled for some bills, and laid them on the table.

'Let's go before we find ourselves locked out of the hotel.'

They threaded their way through dark streets and cobbled alleys, always close enough to touch each other but never quite meeting. As they reached the hotel, Jack following her up the stairs, she found her heart was beating harder with every step. When she unlocked the door of her room, it seemed the most natural thing in the world that he should follow her inside.

She turned on the old bedside lamp and their shadows

leapt into life like giant marionettes dancing across the walls. Dropping her bag on the white coverlet, she turned slowly, feeling her heart trying to escape from her chest. He was so close now, she could sense the warmth of his body, smell the fresh night air clinging to his shirt and skin.

'I guess it's time to say good night,' she whispered.

'I guess it is,' he said.

Reaching out his hand, he touched her face with his fingertips, sending anticipation shooting through her like fire. He tilted her chin upwards and traced a path with his thumb along the curve of her cheek from temple to jaw.

'Good night then, Beth,' he murmured as he drew her to him gently. Now she knew what the ache inside her since that day in the office had been. It had been the desire, the *need* to know if Jack's kiss would still taste as sweet as once it had.

As his mouth met hers, she had all the answer she needed.

Her lips responded to his, desire trailing though her body like warm velvet being drawn across bare skin. Her palms ranged over the firm muscles of his back, exploring almost with wonder, the hard ridges of his spine. Their kiss was warm, tender, and moist, and made her feel as if the breath had been sucked from her body, the bones from her limbs.

His mouth moved to the bare flesh of her shoulders and softly his teeth grazed her collarbone, making her gasp and cling tighter to his body. He kissed the spot he had nipped, to soothe it and she felt as if she'd melted clean away. Her palms slid down his back to the waistband of his jeans, edging down, an inch away from slipping under his shirt and exploring the naked skin that lay beneath.

'Until tomorrow then,' he murmured as her fingers stalled at the belt on his jeans.

Her heart plummeted and she took her hands away.

'Tomorrow,' she whispered against his shirt as they broke their embrace.

Then he was gone, leaving her with only the sound of the waves crashing a hundred feet below and the wind rattling the shutters.

When his footsteps had ceased to echo on the stairs, she unlocked the shutters, leaning out and allowing the breeze to cool her hot cheeks. Despite all her good intentions, she knew her heart was teetering on the edge of a cliff every bit as sheer and dangerous as the one below her window.

CHAPTER 21

By dawn, she'd given up on getting any meaningful sleep so she pulled a tank top over her head, shimmied into her new shorts, and slipped out of the hotel. On the quayside, she found an early morning café that was already buzzing with fishermen and shop workers on their way to work.

After ordering an espresso, she grabbed a copy of *Corse Matin* and tried to find the space to think before she had to see Jack again. The previous evening had begun with awkwardness and tension yet had ended with an intimacy that had left her glowing inside even now. Their kiss, so tentative yet so charged, had made her dare to hope there might, perhaps, be a second chance for them in spite of everything. Dropping some coins on the café table, she jumped up, trying to stop herself from skipping back to the hotel.

He wasn't in the little breakfast room as she'd expected and she didn't dare to hope he was sitting on his bed, wondering, like her, what last night had meant—or what would happen next. Too afraid to knock on the door of his room, she repacked her bag, hoping that he might knock on hers.

When she'd waited as long as she dared, she climbed the stairs down to the reception and checked out, jumping at every tread on the stairs. Outside the hotel reception, a squeal of tires heralded the arrival of Olivier's minivan in front of the hotel. She flew to the door in time to see him squeeze the car between a delivery van and a moped. Then he strode forward, arms outstretched.

'*Bonjour*, Beth! I see you are ready, but what about Jacques? He is OK?'

She returned his kiss. 'I hope so. I haven't seen him yet today.'

Olivier's eyes glinted in the morning sun. 'So, you didn't share your *petit déjeuner* with him?'

She managed a smile. 'No.'

He raised his eyebrows. 'I think Jack must have a very bad hangover, not to have woken and had breakfast with you. Maybe too much myrte last night?'

'We went to a restaurant on the marina and then for a coffee and liqueur in one of the bars, but I don't think either of us had enough to make us miss breakfast.'

'Then perhaps Jacques is just very tired indeed,' he said, fixing his eyes on her face. 'Maybe he is having a, how do you say it? A lie-in?'

She felt her cheeks glowing. 'I think he must be still packing. How's Marisa?' she said brightly, as he stowed her pack in the back of the car.

His face fell. 'Ah, I have some news about that. Marisa is not, after all, accompanying us. We have a new traveling companion.'

She tried to hide her disappointment. 'Oh, and who's that?'

'Someone I think, who is connected with your company. A moment, here's Jack.'

Jack emerged from the hotel reception, his pack slung over one shoulder. His black T-shirt and cargo shorts showed off his long, tanned legs and arms. He was wearing a pair of black Cebe shades and her heart started to beat a little harder.

'Jacques, mate! Beth tells me you did not have any breakfast. You are a little delicate?' teased Olivier.

'As a matter of fact mate, I feel fine,' he said, stealing a glance in Beth's direction. 'I took an early call from Martha, my PA.'

Relief flooded through her. He hadn't been deliberately avoiding her then. He didn't seem to be regretting their kiss.

'*Bien*. Now we have the bags loaded, we should try and leave before it gets too hot.' said Olivier, checking his watch. 'But first, we have another trekker to meet and I hope she will be here soon. Ah. I think this may be her.'

Tottering towards them up the narrow cobbled street

from the town was a tall blonde woman wearing a cream suit and sunglasses the size of welding goggles. The woman waved at them and Olivier waved back. Jack seemed to be struck dumb yet as the blonde drew near, he suddenly burst into a smile and strode forward to greet her. Instantly, Beth's stomach seemed to plunge from almost the highest point of the roller coaster to the very bottom.

'Jack, darling!'

'Camilla,' said Jack, kissing the blonde on both cheeks.

Beth bit her lip hard, hoping the horrible lump in her throat would disappear before she burst into tears. The past 24 hours had been a bubble, as fragile as it was beautiful. It had grown and grown in its brightness and now it had just burst in front of her.

'Hello, Beth' said Camilla, her arm around Jack.

Beth squeezed out a reply. 'Um… Hi, Camilla. What a lovely surprise. Are you on a job for the magazine?'

She puckered her brow and pursed her lips. 'Oh dear. Hasn't Jack *told* you, yet? I'm coming on the trek with you.'

If fate had been kind, thought Beth, a hole in the ancient cobbles would now open up and swallow her. Jack had invited Camilla on the trip. He had been *playing* with her the previous night. 'Oh, I—I didn't realize…' she stammered.

'I haven't told anyone, Cam,' said Jack, looking hard at Beth before turning to Camilla with a smile. 'Because I didn't know you were on the island. Not that we're not delighted to see you, of course.'

'Really?' she asked sharply. 'I thought Olivier had explained everything to you last night. I phoned his office when I arrived at the airport and he said there would be *pas de problème*.' She threw a triumphant smile at Beth. 'No problem *whatsoever*.'

Olivier looked downcast. 'I am afraid that I am to blame. You see, I try to phone you last night but you both have your *portables* switched off…'

Camilla narrowed her eyes. 'Both?'

'*Mais oui*, but the hotel say you are not in your rooms or the bar, so I sent Marisa round to the reception with a note.'

'Perhaps you were too preoccupied with talking shop?' offered Camilla.

'Actually, we were,' said Jack quickly, taking her arm and steering her in the direction of the car. 'We turned off our phones so we could focus on the planning for the trip.' He smiled. 'I'm really sorry we didn't get your note, Olivier.'

'Maybe the porter forgot to deliver it?' said Beth as Camilla pursed her lips.

'Maybe you were so hard at work together that you forgot to pick it up,' she said.

Jack kissed her cheek. 'No matter, Cam. You're here now. Shall we just get on with things?'

'You did say it was an open invitation and when I found from Martha that you'd decided to head out here with one of your staff, how could I *not* come?' said Camilla, stroking his arm. 'After all, the opportunity to get a little R&R and research a feature on one of your tours, all at the same time, was just too tempting to miss. I thought it was a brilliant idea, don't you think, Jack?'

Beth sank a little lower into the stone cobbles as he smiled indulgently. 'It's fine, Camilla. A little notice might have helped us make you more comfortable, but now you're here, we'll do our very best.'

'And how nice of you to write about us, Camilla,' added Olivier, giving her an apprising look.

'It is, isn't it?' she said, treating Olivier to a dazzling smile. 'It's a huge coup to get space in our publication you know. I have travel PR's phoning and emailing me night and day, simply begging me to mention their companies.'

'It's very generous of you,' said Jack briskly. 'But shall we get on our way before it gets too hot?'

Placing his hand on her elbow, he steered Camilla towards the car. Beth's heart was now in her scuffed boots. In her beautifully cut cream suit and strappy shoes, Camilla seemed like a rare and exotic butterfly. Beth knew a new pair of shorts and a few highlights couldn't change that.

'Don't forget to call at my place!' warned Camilla as Olivier rattled down a cobbled street, barely missing some tourists and a girl with a tray of pastries.

'Do you have your own place here?' said Beth in amazement.

'Well, not mine *exactly*. I've borrowed it from a friend. Well, actually he's the publishing director. Besides, you didn't possibly think I was going into the wilds dressed like this did you?'

Just then, she caught sight of Jack in the wing mirror; his face set in an expressionless mask.

'I think Camilla looks *très chic*,' called Olivier, as they whizzed past the sea wall. She clutched the grab handle and wondered if she was going to get her first bout of car sickness since her father had taken her round Scotland in an old Ford Mondeo. Minutes later they were hurtling between the gates of a smart marina apartment block. Camilla exited the car as elegantly as she'd got in and stopped by the entrance door. 'Do you want a quick coffee while I change and collect my luggage?' she asked.

'Thanks, but we'd better get started if that's OK,' said Jack.

'I'll be five mins, darling. You won't even know I've gone.'

Half an hour minutes later the car was still parked in the reserved parking space, and after discussing their itinerary, everyone except Olivier had subsided to a stony silence.

'Beth, why don't you go and see if our guest is OK?' he asked.

Jack nodded. 'Good idea.'

When she rapped on the door, she found Camilla had changed into tailored navy shorts, a white macrame bikini top and a pair of kitten-heeled flip-flops.

'Nearly ready!' she trilled. 'Just need to get my rucksack.'

Beth could hardly miss the pack, lying huge and bulging

on the floor. Jars and bottles and clothes were scattered on the bed.

'Shall I take your bag?' she asked, not daring to mention the flip-flops.

'I haven't finished packing yet,' snapped Camilla.

Beth picked up the bag anyway. 'Would you like a hand?'

Camilla shrugged as she hauled it up off the floor tiles and winced. 'I hope it won't be too heavy…' she said tentatively, worried for Camilla's sake.

'Well, I'm not taking anything out and I absolutely will not do without my essentials. I have my own bodywash custom-produced by a man in Dulwich Village. If I use mass-produced toiletries, I break out in zits.'

Beth saw the determined look in her eye and backed down. 'What about if I take some of your stuff in my pack?'

'Of course, I'm forgetting,' said Camilla handing over three large plastic bottles and a jar of *Crème de la Mer*, 'you're used to this kind of thing. I expect you could carry an elephant and still not be tired.'

Olivier and Jack were sitting on the bottom of the apartment steps as Beth struggled down with the rucksacks.

'Jump in Camilla, *chérie*,' said Olivier, beaming as he and Jack loaded the bags in the car. 'Place your lovely *derrière* on that seat and relax. We will make sure you have a simply marvelous time.'

'Shall we go?' said Jack, stone-faced as he handed her into the back.

Camilla swung her legs into the SUV and buckled up. Jack jumped into the front seat and Olivier revved the engine.

'So, Beth,' she called as they set off. 'How's that boyfriend of yours? The used car salesman? Have you set a date for the wedding yet?'

CHAPTER 22

FUNNY HOW 36 HOURS COULD SEEM LIKE A LIFETIME, decided Beth, as she opened her eyes the following morning to find herself alone in the girls' tent. Next to her lay a crumpled sleeping bag, the *Crème de la Mer*, and the flip-flops. Camilla had been forced to abandon them within an hour of starting the walk and, with the utmost reluctance, had been persuaded to borrow Beth's favorite O'Neill trekking sandals. They were still barely halfway through their trek and by now, Beth was praying that Freya might actually find a transporter to beam her back to base.

Through the nylon of the tent, a high-pitched giggle reached her ears, followed by the rumble of Olivier's deep laugh. She couldn't hear Jack laughing, but that wasn't surprising; he'd hardly got beyond a monosyllable since they'd left Camilla's flat in Bonifacio. When they'd set off on that first morning, Beth had been worried that her illicit kiss with Jack was written all over her face. Bizarrely, she felt like a scarlet woman, but as the shadows lengthened and the heat ebbed out of the day, she was already wondering how close Jack and Camilla really were.

The four of them had spent the morning winding their way up hillsides, through forest tracks and dusky clearings before stopping for lunch by a shepherd's hut. Camilla had initially continued what could only be described as a flirtatious assault on Jack. He, by contrast, seemed lost in his own world, polite when required to be, but focused a lot of the time on his feet or the horizon. Fortunately, Olivier had talked enough for all of them, carrying Camilla's bag and offering a helping hand at slightest opportunity.

When they'd finally made it to their campsite, they'd sat round the fire until the sky had turned inky blue. Jack tried to persuade Camilla that pasta sauce and a few olives were not enough to fuel a day's trekking. After dinner, Olivier had massaged her feet before handing round a large flask of myrte.

Later, as Beth had climbed back to the camp in the dark after washing in a stream, she'd heard Camilla's unmistakable laugh from inside the boys' tent. She'd stood for a moment under the emerging stars, holding her breath, desperate to know which of the boys was actually inside. She must have fallen asleep quickly because she didn't remember Camilla coming to bed.

Beth burrowed back down in the sleeping bag, hoping to block out her confusion with the morning light. When she and Jack had shared that bone-melting kiss in her hotel bedroom, she'd come so close to giving everything to him again. She'd hoped that they could move forward in some way, but the arrival of Camilla had crushed her fledgling hopes.

And yet now… was it possible that Camilla had found a new interest? One who loved dancing attention on her and enjoyed pandering to her every whim? Beth thought back to the previous evening, to Olivier slipping off Camilla's sandals like a devoted subject before his queen. She could never imagine Jack massaging *her* feet like that. God, no, he'd have probably handed her a Band-Aid. She found herself grinning at the image before the rasping of a zip made her poke her head out of the sleeping bag.

'Morning,' said Jack, squatting down in the entrance as she blinked at the light.

'What time is it?' she asked, hoping she looked more composed than she felt.

'Past eight.'

'Oh, bugger. I'm sorry, have I made us late?'

'I shouldn't worry. We're miles behind now. No point rushing,' he said. 'Your breakfast's waiting, unless you're feeling the worse for wear after Olivier's nightcap last night.'

It was the first proper conversation they'd had since their dinner in Bonifacio. 'I'm fine, thanks.' She hesitated. 'I'll be out in a minute.'

He started zipping up the tent flap, and then undid it again, his head reappearing in the flap. 'Beth?'

'Yes?'

'I want the extra stuff you've been carrying for Camilla before we leave.'

Then he was gone. Hearing his retreating boots, she wriggled into her knickers. She could have managed the heavy rucksack again. She ought to be a bit put out, but instead found herself glowing inside from his thoughtfulness. In fact, the little lift her heart gave when he'd spoken, set off a little danger signal.

When she'd tugged on shorts and a T-shirt, she decided to give Louisa a call. She found her phone and waited for the ringtone. It just clicked into the answerphone as she'd expected. Louisa would doubtless by dead to the world at this hour.

By one o'clock, they'd reached the halfway point of the second day's trek and decided to have lunch at a bar in a tiny village. Camilla insisted on going inside into the air-conditioned bar and Olivier had begged to go with her. Beth found a seat at a shady table overlooking the distant coast and tried Louisa's phone a second time. The answerphone clicked in again so she pushed the mobile back in her bag. Louisa was probably out shopping.

'Penny for them?' said Jack, placing a tray with two paninis and cool beers on the table.

'I'm just thinking about home.'

He pulled his chair under the metal table. 'Marcus not phoned?'

She glanced at him, but his eyes were hidden behind his

black sunglasses. 'No. It's Louisa I was trying to call, but she must have her phone switched off.'

'And are you worried?'

'Not really. She's a teenager. She might have run out of credit or her battery's gone dead.'

He pushed his glasses back onto his hair. 'Maybe she doesn't *want* to be available right now. She must be at that age where she doesn't want big sister checking up on her every five minutes.'

'I just… worry a bit that's all. Dad's so busy with the shop and with mum not being around, well…' her voice trailed off. Maybe she did fuss too much about Louisa, but if she didn't keep an eye out for her, who would?

'If I were you, I'd stop fretting so much and enjoy the time we've got out here. Pretty soon, we're going to have to go back to reality and I, for one, am not looking forward to that. Despite the… little hitches, I actually don't want this to end. I'd forgotten how beautiful it is out here. It could turn a man's head,' he said, closing his fingers around the beer bottle on the table.

'Turn it away from what?' said Beth.

'From the rat-race, the eight to ten, the four walls of an office, even one with a view over the whole city. I miss this—trekking, guiding, instructing…'

'I did wonder how you'd been persuaded to join the suits,' said Beth, tentatively. 'At one time, you said nothing on earth or hell would get you into a city office.'

But that was years ago when we were both different people, she told herself. Now she wasn't sure. Their kiss in her bedroom two nights before had persuaded her, for a time, that they still shared so much. Like now, when they were both longing to stay out here. Was that because they wanted to flee from the city, or would they have felt like this anywhere as long as they were together?

Jack took a long drink from his beer then wiped his wet lips with his hand, leaving a creamy streak of foam across his strong knuckles.

'We can't stay away forever,' she said, toying with the salad on her plate. 'I've got responsibilities.'

'We all have responsibilities. Sometimes circumstances force you into taking steps you'd never dreamed you would. Life just bowls you over. Now, I don't know about you, but I'm starving. Shall we eat?'

When they'd finished lunch, she tucked some money under the bill clip. 'Shall we haul Camilla and Olivier out of the bar?'

'Good idea. Shall I do it or will you?'

Before she could reply, the noise of an engine drew their eyes to the road outside the bar. A dusty people carrier had pulled up, its wheels churning a cloud of dust into the air.

'I know that car,' said Jack.

'It's Marisa. What's she doing here?'

He shrugged. 'I haven't got a clue. She wasn't scheduled to turn up.'

Laughter beside them heralded the emergence of Camilla and Olivier from the bar.

'How lovely to see you!' she heard Camilla call as Marisa made her way over. 'You're a lifesaver, darling!'

'Hi,' said Marisa, clearly taken aback by the warmth of her reception. 'You must be Camilla.'

'What brings you here?' said Beth, kissing Marisa.

'Thank you for coming so quickly, Marisa,' cut in Olivier quickly.

Marisa shrugged. 'No problem. Your call sounded urgent.'

'Is anyone going to tell me what's going on?' asked Jack.

Camilla stepped forward, head slightly bowed. 'Well, I feel so awful about this, but I'm afraid I'm going to have to leave you.'

'*Et moi aussi*,' declared Olivier, a rather sheepish expression on his face.

'Um… is everything OK?' asked Beth, thinking that Camilla looked positively glowing.

'No trouble at home, is there, Cam?' said Jack.

She let out a high-pitched giggle. 'God no! It's just… oh, this is terrifically embarrassing, but I'm afraid I've had an offer I can't refuse from the Serene Seas Retreat in Sardinia. They want me at the launch of their new holistic spa.'

'Can't someone else go?' he asked sharply.

'Jack, don't be ridiculous. I'm *Voyage's* spa expert. No one evaluates seaweed wraps and colonics better than I do and besides, I couldn't disappoint…' she whispered the

215

name of a Middle Eastern royal who even Beth had heard of. 'I can hardly say I can't accept his generous invitation because I'm camping with you, now can I?'

'Quite,' said Jack then turned his eyes on his friend. 'But I don't really understand why you have to leave us too, Olivier.'

Olivier shrugged. '*Mais*, I need to escort Camilla to the ferry.'

'Can't one of your other staff do it? Marisa, perhaps?'

'They are all *très occupés*,' he said, looking sheepish. 'And I have an urgent problem with the—how do you say it—the taxman to sort out. It is best we both go back now.'

Beth stood aside, struggling to make sense of her feelings. After she and Jack had begun to build a few bridges again, she was disappointed that their trip was going to be cut short. Going back now meant they'd be back in London and back to a working relationship. She didn't know how she felt about that anymore.

Camilla climbed, queen-like, into the people carrier as Olivier and Jack loaded in the packs, deep in conversation. Beth went to add her rucksack to the pile in the boot, but Olivier shook his head.

'*Mais non*, Beth. You will be needing that.'

'Are we walking back to Bonifacio, then?' she joked. 'I don't mind, but it might take a while.'

Through the window of the people carrier, she could see Jack kissing Camilla.

'Beth,' said Olivier, taking her hand, 'it is only Camilla and I who are returning to Bonifacio. I have discussed it with Jack and he agrees, there is no need to spoil the rest of your trip. You have your flights booked for Friday. The weather is fine, so why ruin your trek? Why not carry on with your research?'

'Olivier doesn't want his problems to affect our experience,' said Jack, back at her side.

'I am very sorry, but we must go,' said Olivier, dropping her hand with a kiss. 'I will collect you on Friday. Telephone me when you are near the rendezvous point. Have a nice trip,' he said then, to her horror, he winked.

'Jack…' she hissed, but Olivier was already opening the car door.

It darted into her mind that Jack had engineered them being alone together, but she squashed down the thought. Now he was standing beside her, waving cheerfully. 'Be professional,' he said through his grin as Olivier got into the car and slammed the door. A slender arm shot out of the rear window as the engine started.

'Bye, don't do anything I wouldn't do!' shrieked Camilla.

Then the SUV was gone in a whirl of dust, Marisa at the wheel and Olivier grinning from the back window. Beth found herself alone with Jack and looking at the kit left on the ground between them. They now only had one tent.

CHAPTER 23

ONE TENT: TWO PEOPLE. EVEN WITH HER MATH, BETH could work that one out. One of them would have to sleep outside. Not that they'd discussed the issue of who was going to sleep where. After their initial exchange at the restaurant, she'd slung her backpack on her shoulders and taken off at warp speed, leaving Jack trailing in her wake. She just didn't want to face the fact that they were going to be alone together for two whole days. The stakes had suddenly become too high to bear.

'So, it's just us?' she said when he'd caught up with her about half a mile down the route.

'Looks like it,' he said. 'Just you, me, and a few mouflons. And before you ask, you can stop fretting about having to share a tent with me, if that's what's bothering you. I'll sleep outside.'

'I'm not bothered about anything. I'm absolutely *fine*.'

He frowned. 'Really?'

Beth tightened the straps on her rucksack ready to set off

again, but Jack still lingered. 'I didn't invite Camilla on this trip, you know,' he said. 'I did issue a general invitation, but I had no idea she was going to turn up here. You must believe I wouldn't do that without warning you first. I've checked with Martha. She says Cam phoned her day before we left and Martha let slip that I was heading out here.'

His explanation sounded convincing enough to her, but then again, so had his reasons for turning up unexpectedly at the airport. So had his kiss in her room back in Bonifacio. With that kiss, Jack had convinced her for a whole night that she was special again before Camilla had arrived and blown everything apart. And yet he hadn't acted like a man in love around Camilla, but... Oh, God, thought Beth, I still don't know him, I still don't *trust* him.

'Jack, it's fine,' she said quickly. 'You can ask whoever you like to come with us. You're the boss, after all. Now, shall we get going? We've got a trek waiting for us.'

He said no more and they set off again, covering the ground much faster without their companions. She had to quicken her stride to keep up with him, as he was setting a cracking pace. With the extra ten inches in the leg department he was bound to have an advantage, but she was determined to match him in every way. No matter how hard she worked to shake him off, she could still hear his size elevens thudding a few feet behind.

By late afternoon, she was red-faced and hot and desperate for a break. A shepherd's hut ahead made her sigh with relief. It meant a spring and some shade. She hauled herself up the last few meters of trail and onto the top of the ridge. When she turned round, he was beside her, looking as fresh as a daisy.

'Want to take a break?'

She nodded.

He handed over a bottle. 'Water?'

She smiled. 'Yes. Thanks.'

Later, they sat in the shade of the hut, her back resting against the stones of the old wall. Jack had stretched out with his head on his pack and soon the rhythmic rise and fall of his chest told her he was asleep. She took off her shades and watched him. Even in shadow, she was close enough to see the scar on his chin that hadn't been there eight years ago. The thick lashes she'd loved so much fluttered against his tanned cheek.

A cicada in a tree set up a chorus loud enough to wake the dead but Jack slept on. His head was turned to one side, one hand resting across his stomach, the other palm up on the dusty ground. As she watched him, he let out a deep sigh then he shifted uncomfortably as if he was about to wake up. Her eyes instantly became glued to the map on her knees. After a few seconds of yawning and stretching, she lifted her chin up to find a he'd fixed a lazy smile on her.

'Oh shit,' he groaned, rubbing his eyes. 'Sorry about dozing off. I must be getting old or maybe I'm just way out of shape these days.' He sprang up energetically and swung his rucksack onto his shoulders, starting to refasten the straps. 'Are you ready to find our camp spot?'

She found herself smiling back. 'Yeah. Sure.'

She gave up trying to race him and finally dropped behind, trying not to focus on his rear view. The tightening and relaxing of the muscles in his calves and thighs as he scrambled up slopes was hard to ignore. She hated herself for what it did to her. Once or twice, he paused, with his hand outstretched to help her up a tricky scramble. She was going to refuse, but found herself taking it. His grip was strong as his fingers fastened around hers. Then he just turned and continued, saying nothing while she clenched and unclenched her fingers, as if she could somehow shake off his touch by sheer will.

The sun was slipping down behind the mountains when they reached the night's stop: a clearing beside a mountain stream. Beth got busy with the tent while Jack started a fire and cooked dinner.

'I wonder how Camilla and Olivier are getting on?' she asked, as he handed her a plate of pasta. 'I mean… he seemed to like her…'

He gave a wry smile. 'I suppose Olivier's the type some women go for, not that I'd know about that.'

'He is, take it from me,' said Beth.

'Really?'

'I mean he's not *my* type, but he's a bit… a bit dangerous I suppose.'

'And is that what women want? Someone dangerous?'

She decided to laugh that one off. 'Only in the movies.'

In real life, she wanted to say, most of us want someone more reliable. Someone they can trust, no matter how risky they may seem on the surface. 'Camilla must come across plenty of dangerous guys on her spa retreats. What do you think Olivier has that's so special?' she added, scooping up a forkful into her pasta.

'Half of southern Corsica, actually.'

'Tell me you're kidding?'

He shook his head. 'Nope. His family has some kind of shipping connections and land. They go back to the Genoans or something. He doesn't really need to work, but he has to do something.'

'Are you telling me Lorenzelli Tours is a *hobby*?'

'Well, I wouldn't have put it quite like that, but he certainly has a good time doing it. He's his own boss, when he wants to play at being one; he spends a lot of his time outdoors and the rest meeting lots of young, attractive women. And he has money to spare to help out the community. He's a very happy man. I envy him.'

'I can see his attraction, but do you really think the feeling's mutual?'

'I think he fancies the pants off her but he's not daft. They'll have good time but Olivier won't be snared that easily, not even by *Voyages* magazine's best spa reporter.'

'Perhaps you're underestimating their feelings,' she said

carefully. 'The two of them went off for ages yesterday morning and, considering what has happened, I'm not sure it was to look for the wild boar.'

He rolled out the deep laugh that softened his face and took years off him. Beth felt herself smiling too, with a pleasure that spread to her whole body, untangling knots of tension, unwinding her resolve to be angry with Jack. It was at moments like these, simple things like sharing a meal, that reminded her why they'd connected so quickly in the first place. They really were two of a kind, both longing to escape from the nine-to-five, both truly at ease out here in the mountains. But that was only on the surface, wasn't it? They weren't alike in the things that really mattered: like commitment and responsibility.

A shiver rippled through her.

He noticed immediately. 'Are you getting cold? Shall I stoke up the fire?'

She shook her head and scrambled round for a change of subject. 'Do you think Camilla will still write a feature on us, after what's happened?'

'After Olivier's sweet-talked her and invited her to the family villa, I've no doubt; she'll be eating out of his hand.'

'Still, who knows what she'll write. It may not be the report we were expecting.'

'I can live with that,' he said, collecting his plate and holding his hand out for hers. 'At least she didn't break her ankle or fall down a cliff. Being pursued by a multi-millionaire can't be that bad.'

He set the plates aside and crouched down by the stove, ready to boil up the coffee. He held up a silver flask. 'Night cap? Warm you up?'

'Is that Olivier's?'

'He thought we might enjoy it.'

She knew she should refuse, but then thought what the hell? One wouldn't do her any harm and she had to admit, anything that helped her sleep tonight had to be worth a try. Because sooner or later, one of them would have to talk about what had happened the other night in the hotel, she thought, as the fire grew dimmer and the sky darker. Soon, the coffee was finished.

'Better call it a day. I'll see you in while,' he said, getting up and throwing the dregs of his coffee on the fire, he disappeared downstream.

She waited a minute or two before wiping out the coffee mugs and crossing to the tent. Their sleeping bags were lying rolled up together at the entrance. She shook out hers and laid it down on top of her bedroll. She didn't have a clue what to do with Jack's and, earlier, had considered leaving it on the ground, taking him at his word that he'd be happy to sleep under the stars. Now she had calmed down, it seemed such a petty and infantile thing to do. She wondered about bringing it into the tent and unrolling it next to hers, but if so, she might as well hold up a card saying she wanted to rip his boxers off. Brushing her teeth brought no solution so she crawled inside and stripped to her T-shirt and pants. The sleeping bag lay at the entrance, still rolled up, lonely and neglected—and Jack would be back any minute.

How long could a man reasonably take to have a pee and brush his teeth, without it looking suspicious? wondered Jack. Both of those tasks he'd accomplished within a few minutes of leaving Beth. Now, as he sat on a rock over-looking the campsite, he was at a loss what to do next. How long dare he wait until she was asleep and he wouldn't have to go through the excruciating ritual of offering to sleep on the ground outside?

More important, how long would it take for him to lose his bloody hard-on? If he was like this just at the *thought* of sleeping in the same tent as her, what would it be like if he actually *did* sleep in the same tent as her? Half of him fanta-sized that when he got back and unzipped the flap, she'd be lying stark naked on the sleeping bag with a come-hither look and a willingness to listen to all the things he wanted to say to her. He hadn't dared to take that kiss in her room any further that night, even though he'd ached to make love to her on the big, old bed. Part of him had regretted even touching her because, while she'd hinted her relationship with Marcus was on the rocks, she was still his employee.

Then Camilla had turned up and everything seemed to have been blown apart. Yet today, alone together, sharing their passion for the mountains, he'd thought that a connection had been made between them.

He kicked at a stone and sent it rattling down the rocks then took his time climbing back up to the camp spot, noticing every night sound, seeing insects scurrying for cover when the flashlight beam caught them in its light. It was sleazy to try anything. He had a responsibility to care for Beth and that didn't include making her life even more complicated than it already was.

As the moon slid behind a cloud, he reached the campsite. He scraped his shin against a stump and cursed. As he rubbed it, he tried to make out the tent and tried to tell himself there was no significance in whether his sleeping bag was outside or in. He knew he was lying to himself: he wanted that sleeping bag to be inside.

Ahead now, he could just make out the dark shape that was their tent. He'd seen no light from inside and he could hear no signs of life either. Which was good. The last thing he wanted to do was come across her in her underwear, no matter how appealing the prospect. Checking that the fire was out and there was no food left around to tempt any wild pigs, he took a deep breath and swept the beam of his flashlight over the ground outside the tent.

There was nothing but a pair of boots with two socks stuffed in them.

His heart beat a little faster as he crouched down and unzipped the tent flap. The rasping sounded loud in the still night air. Something buzzed against his face and he wafted it away impatiently before fully opening the flap and peering inside. A mummy-like bundle was lying on its side facing the outer wall of the tent. He was sure the mummy was only pretending to be asleep. It wasn't breathing the slow deep rhythm of a sleeper and it looked as stiff as a corpse too.

His heart beat a little faster. 'I can sleep outside,' he whispered.

There was a pause before the mummy spoke. 'I don't object to sharing, if you don't. We're grown-ups.'

'Are you sure?'

'We don't have a choice and I won't sue you for harassment, if that's what you're worried about.'

Well, it was hardly an invitation to share some skin, thought Jack as he stripped to his boxers in the dark and placed his boots on the other side of the flap. But it was a million miles better than the alternative. Carefully, he crawled inside the tent, trying to avoid shining the flashlight beam into her eyes. She didn't say anything else to him so he wriggled down into his sleeping bag, faced the opposite way, and tried to think about next year's budget figures.

It was late into the night before he fell asleep and he still hadn't got any further with the budget. Inevitably, their bodies kept touching. Their backsides had ended up pressed together pretty hard at one point. Even through the sleeping bags, the contact had caused him ten kinds of frustration. Later, she had rolled over until their noses were almost touching and he could feel her breath like a kiss against his skin. Her face, so close, brought a lump to his throat and knotted his stomach with longing for more than her body.

As she gave a soft little moan, flung out an arm, and rested her upturned hand on his bare chest, he knew it was going to be a very long night.

CHAPTER 24

'JUST HOW DO YOU STAND LIVING IN THE CITY?'

Beth was asking the question of herself as much as Jack. The two of them were standing on a ridge, looking out over the Tyrrhenian sea to an island floating on the far horizon.

'God knows,' he said.

Without Camilla and Olivier, they'd pushed on after an early start. Beth had got up first, washed and dressed out of sight of Jack, then, by mutual agreement, they'd decided to tackle a different route—one that took them via a high ridge that was far too tough a climb for a novice walker. There were some steep climbs that had your heart working overtime, your breath coming in short gasps. A few scrambles that needed hands and feet and a head for heights. Now they were at the top of it, looking down on the rest of the world. Jack pointed to the distant island. 'Elba,' he said. 'What a place to be exiled.'

'I'm not sure Napoleon would have agreed.'

'The prospect is pretty appealing thought isn't it?' he

said, turning 360 degrees and spreading out his arms. 'I mean with all this two hours away, why do we spend our lives in the city?'

'Because we have responsibilities, I suppose.'

Taking off his shades, Jack turned his dark eyes directly on her. 'True, but when your six months is up, you can go home to the Lakes or wherever you want. I have to build a career; I owe the company and the staff. You'll be free.'

Free? She swallowed hard. She hadn't thought beyond her contract. She might need to work somewhere else to help support Louisa. Probably would have to. As for leaving him for good? Right now, with the two of them sharing all this, she felt she could handle staying. As long as they were frozen in time, with no discussion of the past and no hand-wringing about the future, she could almost live with it.

'It's downhill all the way from here,' he said.

She checked the map and nodded. 'Yes and it's only four o'clock. We've made good time today, so we can relax a little.'

'It helps when you haven't got someone wanting a foot massage and a nice glass of champagne all the time.'

'Or a guide who keeps disappearing to show her the wildlife? I wonder what they're doing now?'

He gave a wry look. 'Maybe I should phone Olivier and find out. That is if he hasn't decided to visit his Sardinian villa.'

'Sardinia?' she said Beth, slotting the map in a plastic wallet. 'Has he got a place there?'

'Three,' said Jack.

'As you do,' laughed Beth, leading the way down to the campsite.

An hour later they were shrugging off their backpacks, feeling pleasantly tired and very hot. Jack stretched his arms out in front of him, laced his fingers together, and grimaced as bones cracked. 'What do you think of camping here for the night, then we can just walk down to the rendezvous point tomorrow in an hour or so?' he asked as she leaned against a rock, reveling in the warmth of sun on her face, the way her whole body tingled with exercise. She scanned their surroundings. The campsite was flat and graveled, on a tiny plateau next to a stream, almost a river that cascaded down over pink and grey rocks. Where the water spilled over the edge of a boulder, it had scooped out pools, some no bigger than soup bowls, some as large as bath tubs.

'It looks great to me,' she said.

'I think so too and there are supposed to be some great swimming places down the valley where the river's been dammed with rocks. That's if I remember rightly. Shall we set up, then?'

As she set up the camping equipment, Beth tried not to dwell on Jack's words. *If he remembered.* Even though she knew they were in a totally different part of the island to their first trip here, she felt overwhelmed by the past. The scent of the maquis, the way the light slanted through the trees, the sound of the river tumbling down the valley. All of it brought to life, in fresh detail, the memory of what had happened between them. She thought those memories had faded away, were fast disappearing, but here they were again.

And Jack was here too.

As she watched him working, the memories replayed again. Almost from the moment he'd collected their trekking party from the airport, she'd been lost. He'd been tall, tanned, and scarily confident. Always encouraging her and the other trekkers to try their hand at scrambling, canyoning, and other activities. Reassuring with those who needed it, gently teasing people who needed bringing out of themselves. By the second evening, she was melting every time he looked at her and turning to mush when he offered his hand to help her up a climb. By day four, they'd kissed and by the end of the first week, she'd found herself in his tent in the middle of the night. The next morning she'd crawled back to her own sleeping bag, her body boneless, her heart about to burst with happiness.

She glanced across at him. The tent was already up and he was standing in front of it, talking to the office on his BlackBerry. Flopping down under the shade of a tree, she pulled out her mobile to try and call her sister. Having switched her phone off for a while to conserve the battery, she punched in the code and saw the little mail icon appear on the screen. Louisa at last, she thought, smiling. Jack appeared as she was about to open the message.

He wiped his hand across his forehead. 'It's still really warm. I think I'm going for a swim.'

'Um, OK,' she said, not sure whether she was relieved or disappointed that he hadn't asked her to join him.

He nodded at the phone. 'Is that what you've been waiting for—a message from home?'

'Not really,' she said, guessing he'd hoped she would elaborate.

'See you later, then.'

Turning on his heel, he set off downstream over the rocks. When he was out of sight, she clicked on the text icon. Her message was not from Louisa and certainly not from Marcus.

> Beth
> Hope u r having gr8 time and working hard on the boss.
> C u soon.
> Freya x

Beth had to smile. Freya was such a laugh.

Switching off the phone, she lay back, hands supporting her head. Above, the sky was deepening to sapphire as the afternoon drew to a close. A bead of moisture slid down her spine and an insect buzzed inches from her face. There was grit in her boots and her whole body ached from exertion. She imagined the cold shock of water against her skin. How exhilarating it would feel to wash away the dust and dirt of the day.

Her thoughts turned to Jack, who by now, would be swimming in the cool of the mountain pool. With it came an image, unbidden, shocking, of his body naked and glistening in the water. It slid into her mind and wouldn't be banished, no matter how hard she tried. In her imagination, he stood there, water droplets running down his chest, over his stomach, and down his thighs. She flipped onto her front. Of course he would be naked. He was alone, it was hot. *He* was hot.

She tried hard to resist the melting sensation spreading through her body.

Jack. Naked. Soaking wet.

She only felt even warmer, drowsy and aroused all at the same time.

After lying on her stomach for another minute, she finally sat up. Maybe Jack had the right idea after all. Maybe she needed to cool off too. If she called loudly enough, she decided, as she pushed herself onto shaky feet, he would hear her and have time to put some clothes on.

'Jack!' she shouted, her words echoing off the white rocks as she set off for the pool.

As she scrambled down the rocks, her legs felt like jelly. She was only going to cool off, she told herself. She didn't *have* to do anything she didn't want to. Almost losing her footing on the unstable boulders, she made her way carefully downhill. The noise of the waterfall that had created the pool grew louder. Soon she caught flashes of jade water through the trees. Her hands were chalky from the rocks and her throat was dry. Suddenly, a few meters below, she caught sight of a splodge of red on some flat rocks. The red, she realized as she drew closer, was Jack's T-shirt.

There was no sign of his boots or shorts.

He must have gone for a walk, she guessed. Shading her forehead with a hand, her eyes sought him. At any moment she expected him to emerge from the trees that sprouted above an overhang on the far side of the pool. Below her, the water glittered invitingly in jewel colors that were ridiculously bright. They varied from olive at the edge, through emerald and jade, to almost black where the rocky bed dropped away sharply from the shore. She couldn't tell how deep it was.

Dropping down from her rocky plateau onto the little beach, she sat down and unlaced her boots. If there was ever a time to go for a swim, this was it, while Jack wasn't here. She pulled off her socks and shoes and stood up, scrunching her toes, feeling gravelly sand between them. One more glance round and she'd unzipped her shorts and let them slither to her feet. She kicked them off but left her panties on.

Her T-shirt was half over her head when she sensed rather than saw a movement opposite. Maybe it was the cry of a bird or the crunch of stones underfoot. Maybe it was a sixth sense. Whatever, it had her tugging her top back down and her heart pounding almost as hard as the water into the plunge pool.

Jack was standing on the tiny cliff opposite her. She couldn't read his expression from here, but she couldn't ignore the crazy, unbidden desire that shot through her at being watched undressing by him.

'Decided to cool off?'

His words echoed off the rocks and her heart drummed in her chest.

'It's very hot. Who wouldn't?' she called, flailing a trembling hand in the direction of the water.

His feet were planted square, his hands on his hips, as if challenging her. Daring her... 'Even if that means you have to share this pool with me?' he called.

'I'll have to manage, same as I did last night,' she shot back.

She stepped carefully over sharp stones to the edge of the water which lapped gently at her toes. 'Where have you been?' she asked.

'Exploring.'

He sat down on the cliff top and stared to unlace his hiking boots.

'Did you discover anything?' she asked.

'Not really.'

The boots were gone now, she could see his bare feet.

'Are *you* going in?' she said beginning to shiver.

He stood up and peered over into the pool as if checking the depth. 'What do you think?'

Whether he'd heard her or not, she couldn't have prevented the gasp that escaped as Jack unzipped his shorts. In a moment he'd whipped them off along with his boxers and was standing on the edge of the overhang. She could have sworn her eyes were popping out of her head. She *knew* her heart was popping out of her chest. Oh God, he was even more magnificent than she'd remembered. Long muscular legs, powerful thighs, a flat stomach, broad chest—the years had only added power to his body.

'Jack...' she whispered, but maybe it was inside her head, her voice seemed so frail and he wouldn't have heard her, because he'd dived into the pool and disappeared between the jade-black water.

This was the point, she told herself, at which she should quietly gather up her clothes, put on her boots, and walk away. This was the point at which she should take her chance and escape, as fast as her legs would carry her, up the hill and back to safety. Even as she said it, she found herself up to her calves in cold water. Even as she waded deeper and gasped at the cold, as water slid beyond her thighs and higher, she knew she should have run away. But it was too late.

Suddenly, his head bobbed up a few yards away from her.

'It's bloody fantastic!' he shouted.

'It's cold,' she spluttered, as the rocky bed fell away sharply beneath her feet. She winced as the pool wrapped her in a chilly embrace and then she was off, moving rhythmically, feeling, tasting, smelling, hearing water.

His body was a pale blur just below the surface. Occasionally he trod water, or surface dived, emerging with his eyes shut and water running over his head and face. She floated on her back, sculling gently, eyes fixed hard on the sky above her.

'There are fish down there,' he called. 'You can see them between the boulders on the river bed.'

When she finally dared to look at him, he looked like a boy with a new toy, his eyes shining and laughing.

'We could have fish for tea,' he joked.

She trod water. Droplets ran down her face and she tried to shake them away. 'I'll work for you for nothing if you can catch one,' she dared.

'You're on,' he murmured, setting off with a firm stroke to the far edge of the pool. He stopped under the overhang where the water was black then disappeared, leaving nothing but a ripple on the surface.

Kicking her feet and paddling with her hands, she waited for him to pop up again. It didn't seem eight years ago since they had spent an afternoon like this. It seemed as if no time had passed. Like they'd just fast-forwarded from then to this instant and all the pain and anger between had never happened. The seconds ticked by and she shivered a little, knowing she needed to keep swimming to stay warm. She called out softly, half laughing: 'Jack... where's my dinner?'

Neither Jack nor fish emerged from the depths.

She sculled round cautiously, expecting to find him behind her or to feel his hands suddenly round her ankles, about to duck her. The prospect of being ducked by him was both scary and sexy. *Very* sexy.

'Stop playing around,' she called, trying to shake away the idea. The waterfall crashed on, but there was no other sound. She realized her heart was beating quite hard.

'Jack!'

Her mind started to race too. There wasn't a sign that he had ever been there. She tried to estimate how long he'd been under. Twenty seconds? Thirty? A minute? What if he'd hit his head on a ledge doing the surface dive? What if he'd caught his foot between the boulders?

'Jack, for God's sake, stop playing around!'

Her legs were kicking frantically now as she twisted in the water. She didn't wait any longer. She swam over to the spot where he'd dived, then she slipped underneath the surface. Her eyes hurt when she opened them and all she could see were vague blurs what—ten, fifteen feet below? The blurs could have been rocks, they could have been someone, it was almost impossible to tell. Debris swirled around her face in clouds as she clawed at a shape and hit solid rock. Her knuckles were sore and her lungs ached as she kicked for the surface, gasping and gulping in air.

'Jaaa-ck…'she burbled, feeling as if the world was going to cave in.

Suddenly, two arms shot out, grabbed her waist, and she let out a shriek.

'Hey, hey! I'm here. It's OK.'

Struggling and twisting, she turned to face him. 'You bastard!' she spluttered as water shot up her nose. She started to cough but didn't let it stop her shouting at him. 'You absolute bastard!'

He wasn't laughing as he grabbed her wrist and pulled her through the water towards the shore. She tried to twist away.

'Where the hell were you?'

He kept hold of her. 'Over by the dam, behind one of the boulders. Beth, I'm sorry I upset you.'

'I'm not upset, I'm bloody furious. I thought you'd hit your head or something. Now I wish you had drowned!'

'No, you don't,' he said, as she kicked away from him into deeper water. He grabbed her again, tugging her towards him. 'You don't wish that at all.'

She tried to break his hold, but realized he was standing on a rock while her feet were dangling. Hot anger filled her veins. Anger at the way he'd scared her and at herself for letting him know how much she cared.

'I could have killed myself trying to save your miserable hide!' she shouted, grasping his biceps and digging in her fingers.

'I was here all the time,' he said as she kicked. 'And if you hate me that much, why are you holding on to me so tightly?'

CHAPTER 25

SHE HAD NO IDEA WHY SHE WAS HOLDING HIM SO TIGHTLY and even if she had been able to give a reason, she wouldn't have got the words out. As he slid his tongue into her mouth, she felt heat blooming in her body and muscles tauten in exquisite tension. Her breasts were crushed against his bare chest and her hips were pressed firmly against his pelvis. She felt her body floating off somewhere way beyond the pool as her mouth tasted him again and again.

Slowly, he drew back his head and smoothed a wet strand of hair from her face and she was lost. Every inch of skin and bone was telling her she needed to have him inside her. She didn't want to talk, she just wanted to live now, in this moment and forget the past, the future.

'What about…' he murmured.

'Please, Jack. Don't say anything.'

His eyes were tender as he pulled her towards shallower water and the soles of her feet bumped against smooth, round pebbles. 'That's a first,' he said, as he led her out of the pool and onto the shore. 'A woman wanting me to make love to her and *not* talk.'

She bit her lip. 'We both know this is probably the worst idea either of us has ever had. We don't have to remind each other of that.'

He slid his arms around her waist. 'And?'

'And I don't care, Jack. I want to do bad things…'

'Even reckless things that you'll regret in the morning?' he asked, pressing his mouth to her neck. 'Like this?'

She felt his teeth graze the tender flesh of her collarbone then nip her sharply. Her reaction body's reaction was instant as the memories came flooding back.

'I won't regret any of the things I'm about to do to you,' he said as they kneeled together on the beach then, peeling off her soaking T-shirt, he bared her breasts to the warm air. He kissed a path between them and flicked a tongue across her nipples. She knew what they were doing was a Very Bad Idea. Be reckless, Jack, she wanted to cry. Make me do something completely irresponsible.

'Beth,' he whispered as she pressed herself against him. 'We can't do this, not here.'

'Don't say that. Please don't say that,' she whispered, feeling him pressing hard against her.

He drew back his head and kissed her forehead. 'I don't have any protection on me.'

'I don't care,' she whispered.

His eyes were dark and tender. 'Yes, you do, sweetheart. Come on, I've got some in my rucksack.'

As she let him lead her back up the rocks, she didn't ask why he had the condoms or who he'd brought them for.

'Do you really want to do this, Jack?'

His eyes burned into her. 'I've wanted to make love to you ever since the moment you walked into my office.'

He knew it would shock her and thrill her, talking like that and it did. She quickened her step and he hauled her faster, making her stumble slightly. Then he was ripping open the flap of the tent and they were practically falling inside. He was yanking her knickers down over her thighs and tugging them impatiently over her feet. She helped him by kicking them off and then he was kneeling between her legs, his eyes smoky with desire. As he touched her, she let out a gasp. Her whole being became centered around that one buzzing spot and Jack's eager fingers. He pressed kisses and soft little nips on her shoulders, breasts, and thighs. Then he used his tongue on her, teasing her until she felt so screwed up she was begging for him to be inside her.

This time, there was no need to cram her fist in her mouth to stop her moan of pleasure as he brought her towards her climax. No need for him not to tell her how fucking beautiful she was and how much he wanted to take her over and over again all night. There was no one to hear them.

So as he thrust his way inside her, not gently like her

first time, but with one firm, swift stroke, she called his name out loud to the whole world.

———

Somewhere in the back of her mind during that long night, Beth knew that expecting to wake up in Jack's arms was never going to happen. Not once while they'd shared each other's bodies during the scented night had either spoken a word about the past or what the future might hold. She knew they were issues neither of them wanted to face.

So she wasn't surprised that when she woke up, he was gone—just like the fantasy they'd shared together.

And this time, she reminded herself, he'd made her no promises.

Dragging on some clothes, she crawled outside the tent, blinking in the light. There was no sign of Jack or even of him having prepared coffee or breakfast. She was searching the plateau, straining her eyes and ears to see if she could see or hear him when her phone rang. It was Lou—and at barely eight too. While she'd been abandoning every rule in her book to have sex with Jack, she'd forgotten that the outside world even existed.

She stabbed at the talk button. 'Lou? Is everything OK?'

'Beth!' wailed Louisa.

She felt her stomach turn over. 'What's the matter, hon? Is it Dad? Is he OK?'

'Dad's all right.'

'Then why do you sound so upset, hon? What's happened?'

'He's getting married,' said Louisa, a catch in her voice.

'*Is that all?*' she wanted to shout as relief flooded through her. She could see why Lou was a bit shocked. She was taken aback herself, but it was nothing to weep and wail about.

'Do I need to ask who to?' she asked.

'To Honor,' said Louisa dramatically. 'Who else d'you think.'

She caught a breath. It all added up. The flowers on the table, Honor round the house at all hours, answering the house phone, her father starting to actually care about himself again. She wondered now how she could have been so blind. He was like any other man and he'd been on his own a long time. He deserved someone special to share his life with.

'Louisa, I know it's a bit sudden, but by the fuss you were making, I thought something awful had happened. Why did you have to worry me like that?'

Louisa went into banshee mode again. 'It's not a surprise, it's totally crap! He's selling the house to Marcus and they're starting some random café thing together. We've got to move into Honor's place as soon as it's all sorted.'

The mention of Marcus shocked her. 'Selling to Marcus?' she said, slowly, trying to take in the news. 'What does he want to go and do that for?'

'I don't fucking know.'

247

She fought to stay calm. It wasn't really her or her sister's business what their father did. But still, she felt like cracks were beginning to appear in the walls she'd built around her. Cracks that were opening wider and wider before her eyes.

'You can't blame Dad for wanting to be happy, and as for moving, I'm sure he can't be selling the business to Marcus. You must have got it wrong, hon.'

'No I haven't! I know I'm right. I overheard them talking about it last night and I asked him and he said he would tell us all about it when you got home. Why does he have to always wait until you're here? Why can't he trust me?'

'He does trust you,' replied Beth patiently. 'But he must want to discuss a big move like this together. I don't believe he would make a final decision without consulting us.'

'Well, you're wrong, cos he has. He doesn't give a fuck about me.'

'Louisa, that's a terrible thing to say about Dad!'

There was a pause and then Louisa murmured. 'Sorry.'

'Look, I can't do anything about it from here and I want to speak to him face to face. I'll be home early tomorrow and we'll sort it out.'

But Beth wasn't sure she could or *should* change things.

'At least try and be happy for dad and Honor,' she said. 'I'll get Dad to talk to us, I promise.'

There was a silence on the end of the line.

'*Louisa?*'

She heard a long, drawn-out sob and her heart pounded. 'Louisa, what's the matter hon? Don't cry, it's not that bad…'

'It… is… that… bad.'

'Please, Lou, just tell me what the matter is!'

Her sister took in a shuddering breath. 'Oh, Beth. Don't be angry. I know you warned me about Greg, but I got drunk one night at the boat club bar. I didn't mean it to happen and he said it would be all right, but it was an accident and…'

Her stomach flipped. Greg. She might have known he was trouble, but she really tried to hold it all in. Really tried to speak calmly. 'Louisa—what are you trying to say? What has Greg done to you?'

'I think I'm pregnant.'

She gripped the phone, unable to make her tongue work for a moment. Lou's voice, small and faraway, crackled on the end of the phone. 'Beth, are you there? Please say you're there…'

'I'm here, hon. Just a bit stunned, that's all.' Which was a ridiculous way to describe the sick feeling in her stomach, the way she'd felt her legs wobble. 'Does he—Greg—know? Have you done a test?'

'I'm three weeks late. I keep meaning to buy a kit, but I'm shit scared of doing it. Oh, what will Dad say?'

Beth had a sudden vision of Greg's body being hauled out of the lake while the police took her father away in a riot van.

'Don't tell him, for God's sake. Promise you won't tell anyone!' begged Louisa.

She hesitated.

Louisa started crying. 'Beth don't tell anyone. I'll just die if anyone finds out!'

'You won't. You'll be OK, Lou-lou. I promise I won't tell a soul. We can handle this together. I'm coming home *now*.'

Jack had crawled out of the tent at dawn and had been sitting by the pool as the sun climbed a little higher in the sky. He was staring into the water and getting no answers from the green depths. A sudden gust ripped across the surface, whipping up tiny wavelets.

Last night had given him almost everything he'd dreamed of. Beth wanting his body, Beth needing him. If he'd had his doubts about her loving Marcus before, he was damn certain she didn't now. No woman who clung to another man that hungrily, who'd needed him that much, could be in love with someone else. The way Beth had made love with him had convinced him she still wanted him. Now all he needed to do was find out how deep her feelings went. He stepped onto the shore and he picked up a stone, turning it over in his hand. Then flung it over the water, waited for the splash, and turned away.

Minutes later, he'd reached the campsite, expecting to

find her still in bed or sitting outside cooking breakfast. Instead, she was up and about, briskly pushing clothes into her rucksack and making funny snuffling sounds.

'Beth?'

She had her back to him and he wanted to touch her, but something about the set of her shoulders, the tension in her body, stopped him.

'Hey there,' he murmured gently.

When she turned and he saw her face, he could see her cheeks were blotchy and wet. He felt faintly sick. He wondered if he had anything to do with her tears?

'I'm fine,' she said, summoning up a half-smile, pushing maps into the top of the pack.

'Are you sure?' he said, reaching out a hand to touch her arm. 'You seem a bit upset,' he said, aching to take her in his arms.

'Just… a bit of trouble at home.'

'Not with your dad, I hope. He's OK isn't he?'

'He's fine. Never been better, in fact.'

His stomach flipped at how beautiful she looked, even with a blotchy face and red eyes. 'Well, that's great to hear.'

She bent to pick up the blue dress to pack it away. 'Yes.'

He gave her a moment, expecting her to fill in the gaps. He didn't want to push her, but she stayed silent as his heart ticktocked away in his chest.

'Honey, I'm sorry if I'm missing something here, but why are you so upset if he's feeling better?'

She twisted the dress in her hands without speaking.

'Is your sister sick?'

Her whole body stiffened visibly. There was no mistaking that signal: he'd touched a nerve. 'No. She's not ill. She's fine too. It's just a bit of family business. Nothing we can't sort out among ourselves.'

'I know you're hurting about something.'

She lifted her face to him and for a moment, he thought she was going to engage with him. He thought she was going to burst into tears and throw her arms around him. He thought she was going to give him a chance to gamble everything on one last throw of the dice. Instead, she shook her head and her mouth lifted in a smile that didn't reach her eyes.

'Jack, it's fine. I just need to get home and sort a few things out. Do you mind if we don't talk about it?'

He saw, heard, and felt the shutters going down before his eyes.

'Are you sure it won't help if you share it?'

She shook her head then touched his arm briefly. 'You could help me pack up. The sooner I'm on my way home, the better.'

For a split second, he was going to throw his arms around her and demand to know what the matter was, but he stopped on the brink. The time for unburdening himself was past. She was clearly worried about her family, for whatever reason. His needs and wants were nothing to her, if they ever had been. For now, all he could do was offer practical help as her employer and, he hoped, as a friend.

'If that's what you want, then so be it. Now, let me help you with the stuff. I'll phone Olivier. If we get a move on we can meet him before noon and try and get an earlier flight home.'

CHAPTER 26

IT WAS ALMOST MIDNIGHT AS BETH FOUND HERSELF outside the front door of her home in the Lakes. The downstairs lights were still on, but no light spilled from the second floor bedroom where Louisa slept. She wouldn't have been home this soon, but Jack had got her transferred to a direct flight to Manchester and sent a car for her to the airport. As the chauffeur had claimed her at the arrivals hall, she'd been choked by emotion at his consideration for her.

'*I'll phone you,*' he'd said gruffly just before she'd gone through to the departure lounge at Figari airport. She'd nodded, but inside she was telling herself she wouldn't hold her breath.

Her father was still up when she got home and insisted on making her a drink even though she'd much rather have headed up to Louisa's room to try and find out exactly what had been going on. Instead, she found herself sitting with him at the kitchen table. Scrubbed clean, it was spread with a checked cloth and had a vase of mauve and yellow freesias in the middle.

'Are those from Honor?' she asked as her dad handed her a mug of hot chocolate.

'They might be,' he said as she sat down. 'You look worn out. We weren't expecting you until tomorrow morning.'

'The boss gave me a few days off after our business trip.'

'You didn't have to rush home. You must have plenty of things you want to do down there in London. Friends to meet, parties, clubs. You don't want to be running back here all the time.'

'But I wanted to get home and see you. Lou phoned me; she seemed a bit upset.' She ran her fingers up and down the mug. 'Dad, Lou says you're getting married to Honor...'

'I am,' he said firmly.

'And thinking of selling up to Marcus...'

'I know all of this seems sudden to you and I was going to phone you when you got back from your trip, but Louisa obviously got there first. I only proposed to Honor last weekend and we were waiting to get you both together, but I felt I owed it to Lou to talk to her.'

'I'm glad you told her first, rather than waiting for me. I'm happy for you and Honor, but, Dad... selling up to Marcus. I just don't understand.'

He sat up straighter in his seat and she could see by the determined look on his face that his mind was made up.

'That's been on the cards for a while. I'm sorry, I wanted to have it all planned out properly before I told you girls.'

He stirred sugar into his chocolate, as she tried to digest the news.

'It just seemed the right thing to do,' he went on. 'The business, getting married. Honor's been good to us since your mum died and when I had the accident, I couldn't have coped without her. I think the world of Honor, she seems to feel the same, and that's why we want to be together. If you must know, I've always had a soft spot for her, yes, even when you mum was alive, though I'd never have let either of them see it.'

Her sharp intake of breath gave her feelings away. She was beyond surprised at his words. In fact, shock was more like it—not so much at her dad fancying another woman, but at him admitting it. At one time, he couldn't even bear to hear their mother's name mentioned, the wound was too raw. Now he could admit to things not having been totally perfect between them.

'I'm sorry. I didn't mean to be such a pain. I do want you to be happy, Dad, you deserve it so much. It's just Lou and me, I know we shouldn't be upset and not after all this time. I know we should be begging a wonderful woman like Honor to come and live with us, it's just… God, this sounds selfish, you see, I remember mum so well still, and…'

Suddenly, she found his hand on hers, squeezing her

fingers. 'It's all right. I know it's hard for you both, especially you, love, because you remember Mum better and you had to take her place for a time, but try and be pleased for us. Try and talk Lou round.'

She grasped his hand back. 'I will. Ignore me, Dad. I *am* happy for you. Honor's a lovely person and I can't think of anyone else I could bear to see you with.'

'Now *you* sound like a disapproving father,' he said, shaking his head. 'You're lucky; I almost took a shine to that bolshy community nurse at one time.'

'Not Scary Norma who was always threatening you with bed baths?'

He smiled and she glimpsed the still-young, hopeful man buried inside. 'Yes. I was that desperate. So think yourselves fortunate she's not going to be your stepmum.'

They sat in silence for a while, sipping their drinks. The old clock on the dresser ticked loudly, as the hands crawled towards one a.m. Even though it was so late, her father looked healthier than she'd seen him in months. He had on a freshly ironed shirt and new jeans that were verging on fashionable. He'd had his hair cut in a half decent style too.

Her mug was drained to the chocolately dregs before she dared broached the subject of Marcus. 'Dad, don't be offended, but I have to ask you about Marcus and the business. Lou doesn't want to move, you know.'

'I'm aware of that, believe me,' he said carefully. 'What about you?'

'It's not up to me. It's your life and Honor's. But Marcus? Does it have to be him?'

'Why is that so bad, love? I thought you might be pleased that it's him.'

'I… like Marcus. I respect him, but I've decided he's not the right man for me after all.'

Her dad sighed and his lips twisted. 'I suppose I'll have to be honest. I never thought he was, love. Not really. I'm sorry it's not worked out for you both and that it's so awkward that he's involved with the business, but it can't be helped. This place is no good for a modern hire business—never has been really. If I sell, we can move in with Honor and open a new unit on the riverside estate with room for a café and cycle hire.'

So, he had it all worked out. 'A café too? That's a bit of a departure from the bikes, isn't it?'

'It's diversity. A good move, in my opinion—and the bank's, more importantly. Honor's going to open a coffee shop and we're going to do presentation nights with a guest speaker accompanied by food and dinner nights for walkers and cyclists. It's a much better location, with free parking, a reasonable rent, lots of space, and we won't be relying on one business alone.'

'It makes sense,' she said, a little taken aback, but also proud at the determination in his voice.

'You and Lou think we're a pair of barmy old farts, don't you?' said Steve, his eyes smiling. 'But we're happy.

You girls are both going to leaving me soon which is as it should be. I'm proud of you but I don't need a pair of help maids. I want two daughters who can go their own way in the world, wherever that is.'

'What about the money for Lou's college course?' she asked.

'Selling the house and business and moving in with Honor will leave us with a fair amount, even after launching the new venture. As for the rest, we'll manage somehow.'

'Dad, I think it's a great idea and I'm proud of you, but I'm still puzzled. What does Marcus want this place for?'

Steve shook his head. 'He thinks he can turn it into one of these trendy climbing shops with a couple of flats above. I don't know—I reckon the village is overrun with outdoor outlets as it is, but he said he had a business plan and everything all worked out. Says his cousin's done it in Keswick. And of course, the flats will sell, whatever happens to his retail empire.'

She sighed. *'I'm sure he has everything sorted.'*

'I know he has the cash and he's offered me a fair price and a quick sale.'

'I know he'll be fair with you. Marcus is a nice guy.' Her heart sank a little. She'd hated hurting Marcus, but in the long run, she knew their parting would be the best thing for both of them. As for Jack… he seemed so far away right now, in every sense of the word.

Her father went on, excitedly telling her of his plans. 'I

don't want the hassle of putting it on the market, which could take months, years even, so a quick sale of the place is great. Honor and me, we want to get the new place off the ground as soon as possible. And you, madam,' he said firmly, 'are going back to your high-powered job...'

She wanted to laugh at the irony but felt too choked. 'Well, I wouldn't really call it high-powered and it's only temporary, after all.'

'I should think they'll want you for longer, wouldn't you? If not Big Outdoors, another good company is sure to. Do me a favor, love, and stay on in London. Live your own life, love, and leave me and Louisa to get on with ours.' His eyes slid to the clock on the dresser. 'It's past one. I need to be up early. I'm going to look over the new unit with Honor if you girls will hold the fort here for a couple of hours.'

Getting up, she noticed, without the aid of a crutch, he kissed the top of her head. 'I've made my mind up and that's it. Now, shall I turn off the light or will you?'

<hr />

The following morning, she found a text on her phone. She opened it excitedly then felt her spirits sink when she realized it wasn't from Jack. He'd said he'd phone her, but he hadn't. The text was from Martha, telling her to take a few days off 'to sort herself out.' She knew immediately who had sanctioned the time off. It was kind of

Jack—professional—but not the message she'd hoped for. She wondered, for a moment, if she should call him. Then she thrust aside the temptation. She'd played that game once before, long ago, and it had only brought pain and humiliation. If she meant anything to him, he had to come and find her, one way or another.

While her father was out, she popped the closed sign on the shop door and slipped out to the pharmacy. When she returned with the pregnancy testing kit, she almost fell through the side door. Louisa was already on the other side, pulling it open.

Her face was red, her eyes wet from tears, and Beth's stomach lurched.

'What's up, Lou? Don't say you've already done a test?'

'No. Oh, promise you won't be angry with me…'

She pulled the door too hastily, seeing a customer nosing through the gate. 'What happened now? Is Greg here? Because if he is, I'm going to knock his block off.'

Louisa's hand flew to her mouth to stifle a giggle.

'It's not funny! Do you know how worried I've been about you? You have to get this sorted and do… something. Have this baby or otherwise.'

'Beth—chill! I'm not having a baby. I came on while you were out…'

'Oh God.'

'It was a false alarm. Must have been the worry over my exams and all the business with Dad. Oh fuck, I'm sorry.'

Beth felt like sinking against the doorframe. 'Don't swear,' she said without any real enthusiasm. 'Oh, Lou, I'm so relieved.'

She followed her sister into the kitchen and tossed the pharmacy bag onto the table. 'I was very late,' said Louisa. 'And I did have sex with Greg. We used a condom, but I thought it might have split or be out of date. I don't trust him…'

Beth collapsed into a chair. 'I'd still like to kill him, if I could get my bloody hands on him.'

'Don't swear.'

Louisa looked serious when Beth glanced up again. 'I know I've been stupid,' she said. 'And I won't make the same mistake again.'

Beth knew she might, maybe not with Greg but with some other bloke, but didn't argue.

'Come here, you total prat,' she said hugging her so hard Louisa gasped. 'What a relief. Oh, Lou, please be careful.'

'I will, I promise, and I've decided, I'm not going to college this October. I'm going to ask them to defer my place so I can take a year off to help Dad. I want to get a job to earn my own money. I'm not sponging off you any longer.'

Beth was startled. 'We'll have to talk about it. You might lose your chance.'

Louisa folded her arms and shook her head. 'Not when they hear the circumstances—Dad's accident and all that,

263

they'll give me a gap year, I'm sure. Besides, there's no discussion. That's what I'm going to do and if they won't have me I'll apply somewhere else.'

Beth was speechless. Louisa had the same look on her face that their dad did, when he used to say 'his word was final.' Like Louisa used to have when she went for an audition or when she'd told them she wanted to go to drama school in the first place. And I'm proud of her, thought Beth, and yet… she rapidly found herself swallowing down another feeling that wasn't so noble. In fact it was selfish and immature and she was ashamed to even feel it. In one fell swoop, she realized her family didn't need her anymore. She was free to do what she wanted and that made her feel angry and alone. But she wouldn't have dreamed of breathing a word to anyone on the planet. So she just smiled, nodded meekly, and let Lou make her toast before they opened the bike shop for the day, better late than never.

CHAPTER 27

LATE SUNDAY MORNING, THEIR FAMILY CONFAB OVER, BETH took off to the village minimarket to get a bottle of wine to go with the Sunday roast Louisa had insisted on cooking. As she walked back up the street, bottle in hand, she saw a car parked outside the house and stopped in her tracks.

It was the latest Jaguar XKR with a personalized plate, a shiny phallic symbol if ever there was one, and, she sighed, probably Marcus's. Well, she told herself, she couldn't bear to face him this morning, not after everything that had happened with Jack. Grabbing a pen and an old envelope from her bag, she scrawled a note and crept up to the front door. Then weighting down the paper with the wine bottle, she headed off in the direction of the fells.

It was cool up on the fell top, even in her fleece. Clouds, white and grey, blew briskly across the sky as she gazed out over the lake from the lee of a small rock face. Her jeans were damp from the grass and, sooner or later, she knew she'd have go back or someone would worry.

She hadn't brought her mobile with her. Now she wished she had got it so she could phone home and check that Marcus had gone. Part of her had hoped too, that Jack might call, although she didn't know what to say if he did. Feeling tears threatening again, she wiped her face on her sleeve, rested her chin on her knees, and took in the lake with one last look. Below and behind her, she could hear the sound of walkers climbing the path, their boots slipping on the loose stones. She wasn't surprised. It was a bright Sunday morning and she'd been lucky to have the place to herself this long even if it was a little off the beaten track. Hearing footsteps closing in behind her, she decided to nod a polite hello and then go back home.

'Is this seat taken?'

As soon as she heard the voice, she knew who it was. The transatlantic tinge was slight but unmistakable. The whole world seemed to turn around her while she held her breath.

'Well, is it?'

Her lungs started working again. 'It's free.'

Jack sat down next to her on the damp grass and stretched out his legs. He had a small tear in the knee of one and, through the threads, Beth could see his skin, tanned a pale gold from the Corsican sun.

'You know, people are worried about you,' he said.

She kept her eyes on the rip in his jeans, not daring to look him in the eye. 'How did you find me?'

'I asked your dad. Once he knew who I was, he told me where he thought you'd be. He obviously knows you very well.'

She forced her eyes to meet his. They were full of tenderness and concern. Full of more danger than she'd ever seen in them before, even eight years ago. 'So that was your flash car outside the house?' she said, her words almost being snatched away on the breeze.

He smiled, a little ruefully, she thought. 'I'm afraid so. I drove up in it this morning. I'd have been here sooner, but I guessed you needed time to figure things out.'

He hadn't even had a shave that morning. Ripped jeans, stubble: she guessed he really had been in a hurry.

'You said you would phone.'

'What I've come to say needs to be done face-to-face, not on the end of a mobile.'

Her mouth felt like sandpaper. 'If you want me to resign, I don't blame you. That's why you're here, isn't it? To tell me it's not working out between us and I'm fired?'

He gave her a look that was definitely confusion, possibly hurt too, but her own heart was so full, she hardly had room for any pain he might be feeling. 'Do you really think that I'd come all this way to do that? You don't know me then.'

'You're right, I don't,' she said with a sigh. She felt his hand slide onto hers and it was warm. A gust of wind tugged her hair from its hair tie and blew it across her face.

He tucked it behind her ear, his fingers brushing over her tingling cheeks.

'Now we're here and there's no getting away from each other,' he said. 'Are you prepared to listen to me and get some things straight? I think I know why you rushed home on Friday.'

She doubted very much he knew the whole story. 'You've been talking to my dad haven't you?'

The corners of his mouth lifted in a smile. 'I have. I'm sorry if It seems like I've interfered again, Beth; I had to get to the bottom of this Marcus thing, no matter what it cost me.'

'What did Dad tell you?'

'That he is getting married to a friend, which you are happy about. That Marcus is buying your father's business, which you aren't. And that, as far as he knows, you are not and never have been engaged to the bloke. And that part, I don't know how you feel about.'

She caught her breath. 'Jack, I did like Marcus. I do like him still, but that's as far as it goes. The last time I came up here, we had what you might call "words" and they weren't the words he wanted to hear. I never wanted to hurt anyone and I really tried to make a go of it between us, but we're just too far apart, and I don't mean three hundred miles apart. Marcus and I, we're just too different.'

'I'm sorry it hasn't worked out for the two of you.'

She rested her eyes on the distant mountains, trying to

slow her breathing, stop her heart trying to take off out of her body.

He shook his head and reached his hands up to cup her face, turning it to his. 'Actually, I just lied. I'm not sorry at all. I wanted it to be over between you and him. In fact, I never wanted it to have even started.'

She lifted her hands to his wrists and gently pulled them down. The time had come to step right forward to the edge, no matter what it cost her. 'But why should you care so much?'

She saw him swallow then glance away from her and that alone told her his answer, whatever it was, would not be simple or painless for either of them. 'I don't want you to work things out with anyone but me, because the simple fact is I love you.'

Once upon a time, when she was young, when he had first walked out and for many months afterwards, she would have walked on hot coals to hear those words. She'd had given up everything she had—home, career, the future—to hear him say them. But now he *was* here, *was* saying them, she couldn't quite believe it. Wasn't convinced, not in the way she needed to be. With her whole heart and soul. It simply wasn't enough.

'Then why did you leave me in the first place?' she said, tugging her hand away out of his. 'Why did you ask me to marry you and then just disappear? Why didn't you face me and tell me that you didn't love me? At least I would have had an explanation, not been left waiting, in agony, wondering if you'd ever come back.'

There, it was out. She'd said it at last after eight years and now he couldn't get away.

'I did love you. I loved you very much and I did want to marry you. But I thought what I felt for someone else meant more.'

The sting of his words was sharp. Now she realized why she had never wanted to stir up the past. Because sometimes it was better *not* to know—not to hear the truth.

'I know I've hurt you. I can see that I'm hurting you now,' he went on. Her throat tightened. Just hearing him say it was twisting the knife. 'I know I can never make up for that hurt, but you asked me to be honest and I'm going to be. It all started months before I even laid eyes on you. Months before the trek. I was in relationship with a girl, a long-term partner. She was—is—called Saskia and we lived together in London for a couple of years after I'd left university. Unfortunately, it didn't last and we split up and went our separate ways.'

She put her hand to her mouth to stifle a sob, but he carried on, determination in his voice.

'I'm not going to sugar the pill about the past. I'm not proud of anything I've done, but you have to believe me. I want you to be sure that what I feel for you now is absolutely the truth. I did care very much for Saskia, we had some great times together, but the relationship was over months before I met you. Nothing dramatic happened, neither of us cheated on the other or anything like that, we just...' He swallowed hard. 'Things just fizzled out, I guess, and we both agreed to end it. You have to trust me on. From then on, I vowed to get on and focus on my job and swore that absolutely no way would I get involved in another serious relationship...'

'But you did!' she cried. 'You seduced me, you made me fall in love with you...'

'And I shouldn't have. I was the trek leader; you were in my care. Right from the start, when you stepped out of the airport terminal, I knew it was breaking all the rules. Do you know what you did to me? What you're still doing to me? You only have to look at me, flick your hair, bite your lip like you're doing right now...' He shook his head, his eyes full of emotion. 'You only have to exist to make want to kiss you, do the most inappropriate things a boss can do and, even back then, you were so feisty and fresh and, to be honest,' he said, with a smile that made her stomach flip, 'so bloody naïve you had me on my knees.'

'I wasn't naïve,' she protested. 'Or perhaps I was, to fall in love with you.'

He nodded. 'Maybe we were both as green as grass, but let's cut ourselves some slack now, shall we? All I know is I had never been so strung up on anyone like you. Honey, you turned my life upside down and I found myself proposing at twenty-six, with a job that took me God-knows-where and you only nineteen with your entire life in front of you. It was completely reckless of me and I still don't know how I had the nerve, but I did it anyway. I *meant* it.'

'We both did. I bought into the dream too, so why did you just walk away? Did you just get scared of the responsibility? If you did, for God's sake why didn't you tell me?'

'I couldn't face seeing how I must have hurt you.' He shook his head. 'No, it was more selfish than that. I couldn't face the guilt. I chickened out.'

'But you hurt me far more by saying nothing. If you'd got cold feet, why didn't you at least see me again?'

'That's something I'll never forgive myself for. At the time, I convinced myself it was better not to see you. I gave myself a hundred reasons why I shouldn't face you. I know now, I have done for a long time, I think, that I should have stayed and tried to explain why I had to walk away.'

'Oh, Jack. I so wish you had told me, whatever the reason. If I could have had an explanation. A reason. Even if you had got cold feet…' she stopped, still feeling the pain now. As keen and sharp as ever.

'I *didn't* get cold feet,' he said gently. 'Beth, you couldn't have it more wrong.'

'How could I have what happened, wrong?' she cried, not caring who heard.

'The day I got back I'd barely had time for a shower when the doorbell rang. I was planning on coming up here to find you that night. Instead I found Saskia on the door-step with a baby. She said that he—Calum—was mine and I believed her. His age, the dates, added up. Her parents had emigrated, she couldn't get a job, she said she had my son, so I married her.'

She let out a big sob and covered her mouth with her hand. She tried not to, but she couldn't help it and imme-diately she found his arm around her.

'I'm sorry, Beth. I really am, but I thought that the three of us could make a life together and that sharing our love for Calum would replace our own. I'm sorry if that hurts you, but Saskia and I, we'd had something once. Not the thunderbolt city stuff that happened to me when I was with you, but I convinced myself we could make a go if it. But it wasn't…' he paused.

'Enough?' she said, her thoughts turning to Marcus.

'What about your…' she was finding it too difficult to say 'wife' and 'son.' 'What about Saskia and Calum now? Do you still see them?'

A shadow crossed his face. 'We split up after eighteen months, then she moved to live with her parents in Australia. Our divorce finally came though a few months ago. Just before we went to Corsica, in fact. But it was just a piece of paper; everything was over between us years ago. We should have dealt with it as soon as we split up, but with us both living abroad, it wasn't easy. Now it's all over finally.'

'But what about Calum? You must miss him so much.

He's your son; Saskia must let you see him—you must have rights.'

'I've no doubt she would let me visit, but she doesn't *have* to. I had a photo last year and he's a lovely little boy.' His jaw tightened. 'I knew in my heart that Saskia and I couldn't last, but being a father was more amazing than I could have imagined and because I loved Calum—still love him dearly—I've let him be. Saskia has a new partner now, Calum has a new dad and—' He stopped mid-sentence and drew in a deep breath. 'Beth, you need to understand. Calum isn't *my* son. That's why Saskia had every right to take him. The truth came out the day she packed her bags and left.'

Her head and heart were swirling. Jack had lost everything—Saskia, Calum, her. She noticed he was crushing a piece of heather nervously between his thumb and forefinger. Her eyes were fixed on the tiny, delicate petals crumbling and falling to the earth.

'Was she deliberately deceiving you about being his father?' she asked.

He shook his head. 'I've tormented myself about that a thousand times. I never had the courage to ask her and I still don't honestly know. She might have, but I doubt it somehow. Maybe she found out when Calum had to have some tests for a minor op. Perhaps she had her suspicions from the start but was too scared to admit them to herself. It doesn't matter now. By then, things were going downhill fast in our relationship and we had an almighty row. The truth came out, I guess I went over the top, she packed her bags and left.'

It took her a moment to answer. She felt like she'd been on an emotional roller coaster ride over the past few months and even now was still being cranked up to the highest point, still not sure if she'd be brought plunging down to the ground again. Her voice, when she found it, sounded small and quiet. 'Why didn't you tell me this before?'

'Would you have accepted what I'd told you then, when you were raw and nineteen? No, that's not fair of me,' he said, shaking his head. 'It was me that was raw. I must have been in shock. I didn't know how to handle what had happened. I had a new life with a partner, a child to support and care for. Once I'd made that decision, I convinced myself there was no going back.'

'But, Jack,' she said desperately, 'if you had told me about Saskia, I'd have still fallen apart. I'd still have hated you. But at least I wouldn't have been left in agony of waiting and hoping. It nearly finished me.'

He let out a groan. 'Christ, I'm so sorry. No wonder you were so hurt and angry when you took the job.'

'I wanted to make sure we could never resume a relationship again. I wanted to make sure you could never hurt me like that again.'

'I don't blame you, and to be honest, honey, I think I'd guessed your feelings for Marcus weren't all that they should be after we had dinner together that night in Corsica. But I wasn't sure and that's why I didn't let our kiss in your room go any further. Then Camilla turned up and…'

She put her face in her hands.

'That complicated things and I knew you didn't trust me, but I'm a persistent bugger, these days, Beth. I've finally learned to say how I feel, even when it's going to be painful and difficult. By the time we'd made love, I'd made up my mind to tell you the whole story, the whole truth about Saskia and Camilla, but in the morning you got that phone call from home.' He tossed what remained of the heather onto the ground. She glanced up, thought she saw his fingers were not quite steady. 'You shut down on me and I didn't know why. I still don't, not properly.'

'It wasn't anything to do with you,' said Beth.

'But you couldn't trust me enough to share it.'

'You were—are my boss, Jack. Don't forget that, because it changes things. And besides, I'd made a promise to someone very close to me. You'll have to trust me on that,' she said firmly.

He nodded and sat for a few seconds, his eyes fixed on the ground.

'I could ask you to marry me again,' he said, quietly. 'But I won't do that because what you need now is time and space.'

Time and space? She wanted to cry. She'd had nine years of that.

'Even if did ask you, I'm not sure you could trust me right now. But please we can start afresh from this moment? I'll have to understand if you can't ever trust me again but I'd really like to try and make...' he went on, his words tumbling over each other.

Carefully, she pulled the shreds of heather from his fingers. 'Jack. Please. Shut up.'

She got to her knees, placed both hands above his elbows, and pushed him down onto the soft heather. He gazed up at her from eyes that were hopeful and unsure, just as they ought to be.

'Close your eyes,' she ordered. 'Then raise your arms above your head and open your mouth.'

Straddling him, she pinioned his wrists against the ground and lowered her lips to his. His unshaven chin rasped against her face, as her tongue slid inside his mouth. For a while, he lay meekly enough, letting her tongue explore his mouth. Then he broke her hold, reached up, and tangled her hair in his hands. His other arm snaked around her body and he pulled her hard against him until she could barely breathe. Her last thought, as she kissed him back, as hard as she could, was that it was a wonderful way to go.

—◈—

'What else did my dad say when you turned up?' she asked some time later as they walked hand in hand off the fell side.

'Quite a lot, actually.'

He had his palm cradled around one cheek of her jeans

when an elderly neighbor saw them and shook her head disapprovingly. 'You're scandalizing Mrs. Holdsworth,' Beth said with a smile.

He squeezed her bottom and grinned. 'I bloody hope so. And no wonder. Your jeans need zipping up properly.'

'Oh hell, I didn't think Mrs. Holdsworth's eyesight was that good.'

His hand was there, already pulling up the zip, ignoring the neighbor.

'What about Dad?' she asked again.

'Well, after he'd checked my credentials—for which I had to produce my business card and undergo the third degree,' he said ruefully, drawing another laugh from Beth. 'He said I must think a lot of you to come all this way from London.'

'And what did you say?'

'I told him I did think a lot of you. I told him I loved you.'

'Oh…'

'And your sister heard me too, judging by the shriek.'

She felt as if she could float above the hills right now. 'You do know I'll never live this down with Lou. What exactly did he say to that?'

'He seemed a bit suspicious of my motives.'

'That sounds like him.'

'And then he told me that he'd kill me if I hurt his "lass."'

'Jack! Be serious. He did not say any of that.'

'I believe the "lass" word was used, but he might have

been winding me up. Beth, do people really use that kind of word up here?'

She giggled. 'Only on the telly.'

Then she made him kiss her—actually it was a full-on, bum-groping snog—in full view of Mrs. Holdsworth's twitching curtains. Soon after, they were standing by Jack's sleek car. Beth she ran her hand over the bonnet and shook her head. 'This is yours, I presume.'

'A boy's toy. Indulge me. It doesn't get that many runs in London.'

He winked at her, then flipped a thumb in the direction of the house. 'You know, you dad's absolutely right. From a business point of view, it makes perfect sense to sell up this place and move to purpose-built premises. But if you're that attached to it, hell I know I'm interfering again, but…' He paused, seeming a little awkward, Beth thought. 'I could buy this place if you wanted me to. Marcus Frayle isn't the only guy with money to invest. I could wave my magic wand if you say the word.'

Beth felt deeply touched and hugged him. 'Jack, I love you and I appreciate the offer, but you don't have to play fairy godmother, so put your wand and your wallet away. We'll manage.'

Jack said no more. He might, he thought, put his wand away or he might wave it in a different direction. But for now, he decided, as he pushed open the side gate for her, he'd keep that part of the plan to himself.

CHAPTER 28

One year later

'So. What do you *think*?'

Beth blinked as she looked in the ornate mirror above the dressing table. Two faces peered back. One was hers and the other's was Louisa's. Her sister was standing behind her, eyeing her critically. She put up her hand to the fine chain around her neck. A tiny diamond heart nestled from the end of it and hung just above her cleavage.

'It's gorgeous,' she said and Louisa's face broke into a smile. 'Perfect, in fact. Thank you, Lou-lou. Thank you so much.'

'You look fabulous,' said Louisa.

She allowed herself a moment longer to take in the face staring back at her from the glass. Her cheeks glowed gently with an iridescent sparkle. Her eyes seemed bigger somehow, and the smudge of eyeshadow somehow brought out the pale gold flecks in the grey. That's what Louisa said, anyway.

She got up to find her sister flopped on the big antique bed. Louisa patted the cover. 'Sit down for a minute. You look a bit jumpy.'

Feeling like a fragile but beautifully wrapped parcel, Beth found a space next to her among the cards and wrapping paper that littered the cover. She took a deep breath in. And out. And in. It was supposed to help when you were nervous, so Camilla had told her. Camilla, Beth decided, was wrong. Her stomach was still fluttering, her legs still felt a little shaky and she still couldn't quite believe she was here.

'Amazing here, isn't it?' said Louisa. 'I never thought I'd get to Barbados.'

She allowed herself yet another glance at the pillows decorated with confetti and the champagne waiting in an ice bucket on the little table. A bouquet of stargazer lilies lay next to her on the white cover. She felt the warm breeze whisper across her skin and waft in the scent of hibiscus flowers.

'Camilla said it came top in a survey of most romantic hotels on earth.'

Louisa let out a low whistle. 'And the most expensive, I expect.'

'I haven't dared to ask. It was a wedding present from her and Olivier. They booked us into the honeymoon suite.'

'I should order more champagne, then, if they're picking up the bill,' said Louisa, absentmindedly rifling through the cards and gifts. Beth smiled to herself. Louisa was gorgeous in her pale blue dress. She'd grown even taller and looked fit after her first term at drama school. Happy too, which Beth put down partly to her new boyfriend, a young actor who had ambitions of joining the RSC.

'Nice gift,' said Louisa, holding up a card with a honey-moon couple strolling along a beach.

'It's from Martha, Jack's PA. She also gave us a voucher for a year's supply of Green & Black's chocolate.'

Louisa picked up a parcel roughly wrapped in pink tissue. 'This looks interesting…' she said. 'It says it's from Freya, Tom, and Shreeya.'

'Hey, that's private!' said Beth, pulling the package from her hands. She pushed it under the pillow, her cheeks beginning to burn.

Louisa laughed. 'OK, OK, Chill, Beth. I won't ask.'

'Don't,' said Beth. She'd already opened the pink parcel at her bachelorette party. Inside was a gift that was *almost* too rude to share with Jack, let alone show her sister. The gift tag had made remarks about rabbits and getting all tingly with the boss.

Risque gifts aside, Freya was getting on well, thought Beth with a smile. She'd been promoted now Beth was working full-time as Big Outdoors' development manager. Almost immediately, she and Jack had decided to come clean about their relationship. While the situation had proved awkward at times, most of the team had accepted it far more readily than she'd thought they might. Maybe that had something to do with the way Jack had mellowed slightly since they'd announced their engagement. Maybe people were just being generous.

Louisa checked her mobile. 'Beth, I hate to rush you, but I think Dad will be here in a minute and I've got to go and meet Honor.'

'OK,' she said, suddenly feeling very much like their roles had been reversed. 'Off you go then,' she added as her sister lingered. Then Louisa gave her a peck on the cheek and said: 'You'll knock him dead.'

She found herself alone again and decided to take one last look in the mirror. Her dress was a halter neck affair, cream and floaty, that clung to her breasts and hips like a second skin. Underneath she wore no bra and what she would have described as a scrap of silk. You really couldn't call them knickers. Jack certainly wouldn't call them knickers when he saw them. She giggled out loud; now she *knew* she was nervous.

As for shoes, she didn't bother putting any on because she didn't need them where she was going. All she'd needed next to her toes was a coat of Louisa's pale pink nail varnish and a slathering of Camilla's ultra-expensive foot lotion made by the little man in Dulwich. It was a shame Camilla wasn't here to see the results, but she was currently in the throes of producing the heir to Olivier's Mediterranean empire. Funny how things turned out, wasn't it?

Here she was, getting married. That was three weddings in one year. First her dad and Honor who had given in to family pressure and gone for the full works in a medieval hall. Beth had made a speech and toasted the health of the happy couple and the success of their new business venture, Mealz and Wheelz. As she'd raised her glass to them, she knew she wouldn't have to worry. Apart from the cheesy name, it was all going very well. Her father was looking and acting like a new man and as for the business... with her and Jack as joint investors and advisers, the prospects for the cycling gastro-café were looking bright. Even Marcus had sent a good luck card for the opening. According to village gossip, he was dating a glamorous redhead who ran an off-road driving school.

A few months after Steve and Honor had tied the knot, she and Jack had flown out to Corsica for the wedding of Camilla and Olivier. Now she'd resigned her job, was in love and settled, *Voyages*'s former leading spa correspondent had mellowed surprisingly. At the wedding, a quaint affair in a hill-top church followed by a huge feast on the grounds of one of Olivier's villas, Camilla had actually sought her out and offered her congratulations on her engagement to Jack. Later, as Camilla had steadfastly refused all offers of Krug, Beth was one of the privileged few guests to know why.

As for the third wedding of the year, it was smallest, the quietest, and...

'Are you ready?' asked her father, popping his head around the open French doors.

She picked up her bouquet and nodded. 'I think so.' Then she stepped out of the room and onto the beach.

'You look beautiful love,' said Steve, taking her arm. At least that's what she thought he'd said, for he hardly seemed able to get the words out. She glanced at him, mouthed a thank you, and took his arm.

Between her toes, the creamy-white sand felt warm and almost unbearably soft. A few yards ahead, the sea glittered in the fierce tropical sunlight. The sand changed to wood, sun-bleached and polished smooth by thousands of feet. Through the tiny gaps in the slats, the sea swirled like a turquoise milk shake and above, a tiny cloud slid across the sun. Jack was standing at the end of the jetty, looking, she thought, pretty nervous himself, and her heart did an impressive double somersault.

'Feeling OK?' said her dad.

'Just fine.'

'Then I'll stand aside,' he said and unhooked his arm from hers. He took his place by Honor, who smiled encouragingly. Louisa, standing by, looked about as awe-struck as Beth had ever seen her. Just then, the sun came out from behind the cloud, the breeze stirred the flower in her hair, and she blinked again. What if this whole idyllic scene suddenly evaporated before her?

But he was still there, holding out his hand, his eyes full of tenderness and desire.

'What were you waiting for?' he murmured, as his

fingers fastened firmly around her hand and he brushed his lips against hers.

'For this,' she whispered. 'Only this.'

ACKNOWLEDGMENTS

Firstly, I have to give a massive thanks to the 'travel guru,' Julie Haggar, for her insight into the travel industry and also to Sarah Quee for advice on adventure holidays in Corsica. To Charlotte Houldcroft for reading the manuscript tirelessly, introducing me to The Killers, and helping me shop in the name of research. To Rosy Thornton and Broo Doherty for their endless encouragement, and to Catherine Cobain at Headline for waving her magical editorial wand.

Finally, to John for always understanding and often bringing me biscuits.

ABOUT THE AUTHOR

Phillipa Ashley studied English Language and Literature at Oxford University before working as a freelance copy-writer and journalist. She lives in an English village with her husband and daughter. Visit www.phillipa-ashley.com.

READ ON FOR AN EXCERPT FROM

It Should Have Been Me

PHILLIPA ASHLEY

COMING DECEMBER 2011
FROM SOURCEBOOKS LANDMARK

CHAPTER 1

CARRIE BROWNHILL WAS STANDING OUTSIDE THE STAGE door of the Starlight Theatre wondering how to respond to her friend's outrageous comment.

'So. What would you actually do if Huw had an affair?' Rowena asked again.

Carrie paused longer than she should have done before answering, partly because her teeth were chattering with the cold but also because the prospect of her fiancé, Huw, shagging another woman was something she'd never even dreamed of. 'You mean if I actually *caught* him with someone else?' she said.

'Well, I don't mean in the act, with his pants round his ankles,' said Rowena, in between puffs on her cigarette. 'I just wondered what you'd do if you found out he was dipping his wick on the other side of the fence.'

'Oh, blimey. I don't know,' said Carrie, stamping her feet to keep warm. It wasn't surprising she was freezing, because (a) it was February, and (b) she and Rowena were dressed like fifties tarts. They were taking a break from a dress rehearsal for the local drama society's production of *Grease*. One of the Pink Ladies had set fire to her wig which had triggered the smoke alarms and sent the director into a hissy fit. It had also given Rowena the chance for a sneaky fag.

'Now come on, honey. Would you be calm and dignified or turn into the vengeful bitch from hell?' drawled Rowena, getting into the part of her character, Rizzo, but managing to sound more like Marge Simpson.

'Oh, calm and dignified, of course,' simpered Carrie, pretending to be Sandy.

Rowena took a long, slow drag on her ciggie, then blew out a smoke ring. 'Bull *shit*, honey.'

'Okay. Maybe you're right. If I caught Huw with another woman, I'd probably go totally berserk and wreak vengeance on him.'

'What? Pour paint stripper over his car?' said Rowena, flicking her ash into a tub of winter pansies.

Carrie feigned horror. 'The Range Rover? My God, no. I love that car. It's my baby. I couldn't hurt it.'

'Cut up all his clothes, then?'

Carrie thought for a moment, then felt her mouth stretch in a smile of glee. 'No. Way too clichéd. I'd make the punishment fit the crime. Hit him where it really hurts.'

'You don't mean you'd do a Bobbitt?' gasped Rowena.

'Oh, much worse. I'd pour sugar in the fuel tank of his Massey Ferguson.'

'His *what*?'

'His Massey Ferguson. It's his new tractor. He adores it. He said he'd like to shag me in it.'

'You farming types are all pervs,' declared Rowena, throwing her fag end on to the flagstones and grinding it out with her foot. 'Ow. Buggering hell. I've just burnt my bloody foot! These ballet pumps are as old as the hills.'

Carrie laughed as Rowena hopped about cursing cheerfully. The two of them had been friends since uni, where they'd both studied English and Drama. Now they were stalwarts of the local drama society in Packley, the Oxfordshire village where they both lived. Carrie had met Huw at university too, and they'd been together ever since. She'd once dreamed of appearing in the West End but had ended up helping him run his farm business instead. It was a full-time job just keeping up with all the admin while he managed the dairy herd and small business units at the farm. But if she ever had a pang of regret about not making it in professional theatre, she felt the rest of her life more than made up for it. She knew she'd never have to sabotage Huw Brigstocke's beloved tractor, slash his clothes or wreak vengeance on him. In two weeks' time, she and Huw were getting married at Packley church. Everyone was coming. The drama society, the Young Farmers, their university friends, at least half the village— it felt like half the county in fact, because Huw's mother knew absolutely *everyone*.

'Carrie? Rowena?' A vision in pink peeped nervously round the door of the theatre.

'Out here, Hayley,' said Carrie.

'I just came to warn you that we're ready to start again and Gina's been looking for you. She's already ballistic that I set off the fire alarm,' said Hayley, shivering in her Pink Ladies outfit.

'Gina is the love child of Simon Cowell and Attila the Hun,' declared Carrie, picturing the show's director searching the theatre for her and Rowena like a head-mistress looking for girls smoking in the bogs. 'Can't a leading lady have some privileges? Tell her I'm just taking a call from Hollywood. Tell her,' she said dramat-ically, 'that George Clooney has asked me to play the part of Scarlett O'Hara in his new remake of *Gone with the Wind*.'

Rowena let out a giggle.

'It's okay, Hayley. I'm coming,' said Carrie, finally taking pity on Hayley, who was so naïve she might actually tell Gina what Carrie had said.

'I expect Gina will be on the warpath for the rest of the night now because we've sloped off,' grumbled Rowena.

Carrie flounced towards the door, flinging back her hair like Scarlett would have done. 'Frankly, darling, I don't give a toss!'

A week later, Carrie was belting out the show's finale to a packed theatre.

'*You're the one that I want…*'

'More! More! More!' chanted the audience.

Carrie went for the big one. '*The one that I waa-nnt!*'

The audience leapt to their feet, stamping the floor and almost shaking the roof off the theatre.

'Listen to that,' hissed Rowena as they made their bows. 'Don't you just bloody love it!'

Carrie felt like a giant pink bubblegum about to pop with joy. Every night had been a sell-out and a roaring success, and if her voice was on its last legs, she didn't care. They might not be in the West End, they might only be amateurs, but they were bloody good ones. The curtain dropped and the girls chattered excitedly as they dashed off stage.

'Let's get changed and get to the bar. I need an urgent dose of spritzer and Huw can pay for it. I tried to spot him in the audience but he must have been right at the back.'

'Knowing Huw, I'll bet he's waiting now, with one of those totally clichéd bouquets he's always sending you,' said Rowena.

Carrie sighed dramatically. 'I just hope he's bought red roses this time. Yellow ones are so-ooo passé, darling.'

She wouldn't really mind if they were yellow roses, or even a bunch of dandelions. All she wanted was to see Huw, who had promised to be at her final performance even if it did mean calling in en route from his stag weekend. In fact, she wouldn't mind if he turned up half naked with a ball and chain round his ankle, just as long as he'd made the show somehow. This had been her final performance as Carrie Brownhill; the next programme would have her new name in it: Carrie Brigstocke. Tonight was special in so many ways; she couldn't wait to hear what he'd thought of her performance.

'I hope *Oxfordshire Life* send a reporter to the wedding,' she said.

Rowena mumbled a reply through a face full of cleansing cream. 'I should think it will be picked up by the nationals. You might end up in *Hello!*.'

'Now you're taking the piss, Rowena,' laughed Carrie.

'Would I?'

'Yes, you would.'

Ten minutes later, Rowena was handing over a drink as Carrie scanned the packed bar for Huw's unmistakable profile. He was normally easy to spot, even in a crowded room. Six foot five in his stockinged feet, a shock of thick sandy hair and shoulders like Hercules. Stooping slightly because he was self-conscious, of course.

That was what she'd first fancied about him when they'd met at their university freshers' disco: that combination of capable shoulders and self-deprecation. She never could resist a man who didn't know how sexy he was. Flashy blokes turned her right off, but Huw, who'd braved the laughter of the entire rugby club to ask her to dance, had won her heart straightaway. She still remembered their first shag in his tiny student room, the ancient water pipes creaking and the sound of the rugby club belting out 'Roll Me Over in the Clover' from the students' union.

Over by the bar, she caught sight of Rowena batting her eyelashes at a strange man with a fake tan and an outrageous toupee. Pulling her mobile from her handbag, Carrie checked the screen. No message from Huw. Yet he'd promised faithfully to be here tonight. He always managed to make her last nights, had never missed one except for the time Millicent had had a Caesarean and he'd had to stay with the vet. Carrie hadn't really minded; the herd came first, and anyway she'd been crap that evening.

Rowena returned. 'Who's your friend Wiggy?'

'Oh, just one of my many fans. He said he thought I'd put in a performance of poignancy and vitality, a combination he'd rarely seen in amateur theatre.'

'Bloody hell. Does he want to get your knickers off?'

Rowena frowned, seemed almost offended but then grinned and declared, 'Doesn't everyone, darling? Has Lover Boy phoned yet?'

Carrie was puzzled at the sudden change of subject but dismissed it. Everyone was tired and overemotional. She shook her head. 'No. Not even a text.'

'Maybe he's decided to stop off at the Red Lion for a nightcap on his way home from London.'

'He promised he'd be here for the play. I wouldn't mind but he's already had a two-night bender in London with his mates. How long should a stag party last?'

'Depends who he's met,' said Rowena.

Carrie snorted. 'How can he have met anyone?'

'Well, I know the concept is hard to grasp, but you never know, he could have decided to grab his last chance to escape and run off with a Serbian lap dancer.' Rowena's eyes glinted wickedly.

Carrie laughed. 'Well, if he has run away, I hope she likes his cold feet in bed.'